THEIR CHRISTMAS ANGEL

BY
TRACY MADISON

MILLS & BOON

First Published in Great Britain 2017
By Mills & Boon, an imprint of HarperCollins*Publishers*
1 London Bridge Street, London, SE1 9GF

© 2017 Tracy Leigh Ritts

ISBN: 978-0-263-92347-6

23-1117

Our policy is to use papers that are natural, renewable and recyclable products and made from wood grown in sustainable forests. The logging and manufacturing processes conform to the legal environmental regulations of the country of origin.

Printed and bound in Spain
by CPI, Barcelona

Tracy Madison is an award-winning author who makes her home in northwestern Ohio. As a wife and a mother, her days are filled with love, laughter and many cups of coffee. She often spends her nights awake and at the keyboard, bringing her characters to life and leading them toward their well-deserved happily-ever-afters one word at a time. Tracy loves to hear from readers. You can reach her at tracy@tracymadison.com.

To my mother, for the strength and courage you have always shown. Thank you!

Chapter One

Cotton-puff snowflakes shimmered in the glow of the neighborhood's streetlights as they lazily dropped from the sky. A pretty sight, Parker Lennox thought—the way they twirled and whirled in the air with gentle, perfect grace reminded him oddly of the ballets his late wife used to drag him to when they lived in Boston.

Hard to believe that the last ballet Parker attended was over seven years ago now, and that Bridget had been gone for close to six. Didn't seem possible some days. Other days—like today—those six years were akin to an entire lifetime. Either way, he missed his wife.

Everything about Bridget, Parker missed. Her wide, effortless smile, her laugh—sometimes sweet and quiet, other times chortling and boisterous—the way she would look at him from across a room and how her body spooned into his while they slept.

Lord. *Six* years. How had that even happened?

In that time, he'd packed up his two young daughters, Erin and Megan, and moved them to his hometown of Steamboat Springs, Colorado, to settle and get away from the constant memories of Bridget. Remaining in Boston, with the same restaurants and parks and shops and, well, the same *everything*, let alone living in the house they'd shared as a family, had quickly become an act of torture. For him, but more important, for his daughters.

Erin had been only four, Megan two, when Bridget's cancer won its long-fought, grisly battle. The aftermath of losing their mother had left his little girls in a somber, colorless world filled with pain and heartache. Him, too, naturally, but age made a huge difference in how a person processed grief. As an adult, he knew he had to push through the darkness of Bridget's death in order to find whatever light existed at the other end.

His girls, though? They did not understand this, and the morning Parker had found Erin and Megan huddled together in his bedroom closet with their mother's clothes wrapped around their small, slender bodies and tears coursing down their cheeks had made that fact crystal clear.

That morning had ended his ongoing mental debate on whether they should stay in Boston, where the familiar could, over time, prove healing, or relocate to Steamboat Springs, where the girls might find breathing—just breathing—a little easier. So, despite his mother- and

father-in-law's objections and just shy of a year following his wife's passing, Parker sold his house, quit his job
and brought his family here, to a less expensive home
and new surroundings.

And in the five years since, he'd doubted this decision only once. A skiing accident had come too damn
close to taking his life and leaving his precious daughters as orphans. In those precarious seconds and minutes after the accident, and during those first awful few
weeks in the hospital, his choice to move had seemed
foolhardy. If they'd stayed in Boston, he likely would
not have found himself twisted in a broken heap halfway down a friggin' mountain.

Fortunately, he'd survived, and another three years
had somehow elapsed, along with a multitude of other
positive and affirming changes. His girls were flour-
ishing here, and Parker's momentary doubt had long
since faded into nothingness. Steamboat Springs had
become more than a new place with new surroundings.
They had created a home here, in every way possible.

But yeah, the damn dancing snowflakes reminded
him of those ballets and, therefore, his beautiful, loving
wife. The good—the glorious years they were lucky
enough to spend together—and the bad, the years
since, the years that cancer stole from his family.

Sighing, Parker stopped at a red light about three
blocks from the elementary school and yanked himself
to the present. Two hours ago, he'd driven this exact
path to pick up his daughters and take them to dinner. Now they were returning to the school for the up-
coming Christmas play tryouts. Afterward, they'd go

home and finish their evening routine, and since it was a Friday, he'd let the girls stay up a bit later than normal. Then he really should put in a few more hours of work, otherwise he'd have to fit it in over the weekend.

In Boston, he'd supervised the marketing department of a large national corporation. Ever since their move, though, Parker had worked for himself. In the beginning, he focused solely on designing websites, blogs and the like, but due to his clients' needs, he had eventually broadened his scope to include a range of internet marketing services.

Finances during those first few years were rough, but he budgeted every penny of Bridget's life insurance benefit, along with what was left over from the sale of the Boston house after buying their home here, in order to make the transition a success. He used the living room, kitchen, his bedroom and sometimes— specifically the nights either Erin or Megan were ill or having trouble sleeping—the hallway outside their door as his roaming office. Didn't matter, really, where he worked. To him, the point was that he was at home. With them.

And he continued to work entirely from home until his youngest daughter, Megan, was firmly settled in first grade. By then, Parker's business was solvent enough to rent actual office space about three miles from the school. Most of the time, he managed to complete his work responsibilities during their school hours, but every now and then—like tonight—he'd finish one project or another at home, using his laptop and the kitchen table as his desk.

Life was busy, but good. Oh, there were the stray melancholy moods that elicited memories of his wife, along with the random bursts of loneliness that sometimes popped into being, but Parker was grateful that he had nothing of true merit to complain about.

Thanksgiving was a mere two weeks away, and he had so very much to be thankful for. His daughters were healthy. He was healthy. They had food on their table every night, a roof that didn't leak over their heads, sufficient funds in the bank account, friends and family to cherish, and plenty of activities to keep them involved and happy. Other than the impossible wish of having Bridget back in their lives, what else could he want?

Braking again, this time at a stop sign, Parker glanced in the rearview mirror and said, "Almost there now, girls. Are you excited?"

"Yes!" said eight-year-old Megan from the back seat. "I can't wait! I want to be one of the angels! But so does Erin. Do you think both of us can be picked for angel parts?"

"Don't be silly, Megan," said ten-year-old Erin, offering her opinion in her typical to-the-point fashion. "There's lots of angels in the play, so of course we can both be angels."

"Only if we're chosen," Megan argued. "Only if we're good enough."

"Well, I guess I don't know if *you're* good enough, but I am. So maybe I'll be one of the angels and you'll be a…a…star or a tree or—"

"Daddy!" Megan squealed, interrupting her sister.

"Erin's being mean! And besides that, she's wrong. If only one of us can be angels, it will be me because... because I have blond hair, like angels are supposed to!"

"Angels can have any color of hair, even red," Erin fired back, her voice indignant. "And telling the truth isn't the same thing as being mean! And I didn't say you weren't good enough to play an angel, Megan. I said that I didn't know if you were. That's different!"

"Girls, stop," Parker said, crossing the sleepy intersection and driving toward the school parking lot, which was about a half a block straight ahead. "Hair color doesn't matter at all. And you're both good enough, but that doesn't mean you'll get the parts you want." Every kid who showed tonight would be involved in the play, in one way or another. Whether that would be as an angel, a star, a tree, some other part, or helping behind the scenes. "Let's try to remember that the goal is to have fun and celebrate Christmas. Okay?"

The girls were silent for a few seconds before a muffled chorus of "Okay, Daddy," reached his ears. He hoped either they'd both be cast as angels or neither would, otherwise keeping the peace for the next six or so weeks would become highly difficult.

On the other hand, he supposed if such a scenario were to happen, it would provide a valuable life lesson that the girls would eventually have to learn. He just hated any possibility that brought so much as a lick of pain or disappointment to his daughters. In his estimation, they'd already faced their fair share of heartbreak in their young lives. If the choice was his, Parker would move heaven and earth to keep Erin and Megan from experiencing another drop of sadness. He couldn't, naturally, but the wish remained.

"Oh! Look, Erin," Megan said as they approached the school, "is that a—"

"Watch out, Daddy!" Erin hollered. "Don't hit the angel!"

Don't hit the...what? But her words, along with her volume and the frightened quality of her tone, shocked Parker into a state of alert awareness, and his heart leaped to his throat as he saw that, yes, an angel—or rather, a woman dressed as an angel—was barreling at top speed from the sidewalk to the street, in chase of some type of large, fast-moving animal. A dog? Maybe, but the beast seemed to have horns, so he couldn't say for certain.

Acting on instinct and adrenaline, Parker muffled a curse and swerved slightly to the left, in the opposite direction of the halo-adorned female, while simultaneously braking the car. He would not be father-of-the-year if he ran over a friggin' angel, especially with his daughters—both of whom were now yelling, "Daddy! Stop! Please stop!"—as witness.

God must have tuned in at the exact right second, because several blessed events happened in quick succession. One, he managed to stop the car without too much hassle and he did not hit the woman or the runaway creature. Two, the left-hand side of the road—where half of his car now resided—stayed miraculously free of oncoming vehicles.

Parker inhaled a long, stabilizing breath and put the car into Park. The angel-woman now stood almost directly in front of him, and the car's headlights illuminated her startled expression and rounded eyes. She wrapped her arms around herself and her lips moved in an expletive that Parker identified without being able to hear her voice. Lord. That was close.

Mirroring his thoughts, Megan said in a hushed and somber voice, "I can't believe you almost killed a beautiful angel, Daddy. That would've been so bad. Very, very, *very* bad. The police would probably have put you in jail! And thrown away the key! And…and—"

"Look at her again, Megan," Erin said. "She's not a real angel. She's close enough now that I can see it's really Miss Bradshaw."

"Oh! It is Miss Bradshaw," Megan said. "Why does she look like an angel?"

"I bet she's dressed that way for the tryouts," Erin said. "So Daddy almost killed our music teacher, not an angel. That would've been bad, too, because she's really great."

"Yeah! Really bad!" Megan chimed in. "We love Miss Bradshaw!"

Hmm. This woman was the new music teacher? Why didn't he remember meeting her at the school's open house last month? He always made a point of talking to the girls' teachers, to explain about Bridget in the hopes of avoiding confusion, but Erin hadn't felt well—the beginnings of a cold—and Megan's excitement level had skyrocketed through the roof that night. Those two hours had passed swiftly, and no…Parker wasn't sure if he'd met Miss Bradshaw.

"I did not almost kill anyone, angel or teacher,"

Parker said, unbuckling his seat belt. Even if he had hit her—and yeah, thank God he hadn't—he'd been driving slow enough that it was unlikely a collision would've caused life-threatening injuries. Probably, anyway.

He could've hurt her, though, and it did not matter in the slightest that the woman—Miss Bradshaw—should have known better than to run pell-mell into a street, especially at twilight. The possibility of what could've occurred made him sick to his stomach.

"But you might have," Erin said, "if you'd hit her with the car."

"But I didn't," Parker replied.

"Yeah, Erin. He *didn't*!" Megan added.

"Well, I know that, Megan. I do have eyes, you know!"

"Wait here, girls," Parker said, breaking into their almost argument. "Let me make sure your angel-teacher is okay, and then—"

His jaw slammed shut as Miss Bradshaw, in attempting to walk toward his side of the car, slipped and lost her balance. She landed on the ground, bounced to her feet instantly and scowled while wiping the snow from her behind. Ouch, that had to hurt. And again, she mouthed an expletive that he easily identified without the benefit of sound.

"Wait here," he repeated, flipping on the emergency lights. Once he knew that she wasn't hurt in any way, he had to get his car out of the wrong lane of traffic. "I'll only be a second."

By the time he exited the car, she'd moved closer and

was standing only a few feet from where he stood. "I'm so, so, *so* sorry," she said in rushed syllables as they came face-to-face. "Roscoe—that would be my dog—got loose, and I…well, I was only thinking of catching him before he got too far away or hurt. I wasn't thinking about the road at all."

And oh, if ever a living and breathing human could actually *be* an angel, it was this woman. She was as close to fitting the description of *ethereal* as Parker had ever seen, with her long, pale blond hair, thickly lashed eyes—green, he thought, but he'd require better light to be 100 percent positive—full mouth and the gentle, almost-delicate arc of her cheeks.

A white, ankle-length and cinched-at-the-waist dress—complete with wings attached to the back—didn't hide her curvy figure, and while he had no idea if she wore high heels or flats, he guessed she couldn't be taller than five feet plus an inch or three. There wasn't any way he wouldn't remember this woman, so no, Parker had not met her during the open house.

"Are you okay?" Parker asked, vastly more concerned in establishing her welfare before worrying about her dog's, who seemed to be long gone. "Not feeling faint or anything, are you?"

"A little shaken, but that's to be expected. Again, I'm so sorry for almost running smack into your car." She shivered from the cold, her fall or the near collision with his car. Or, Parker supposed, all three. Angling her body, she scanned the stretch of sidewalk and houses across the street from the school. "But you should probably move your car and I need to find my dog."

"I… Right. Of course, but I'd like to help. Let me get my kids situated in the auditorium and I'll come back out." He noticed with some humor that the band around her forehead had slipped, causing her halo to droop and giving her the appearance of a disheveled angel. It was, Parker decided, fairly adorable. She shivered again and her teeth chattered, so he took off his jacket. "Here, wear this," he said, handing her the coat, "before you freeze to death."

For whatever reason, he expected her to argue, but she didn't. She surprised him with a grateful smile and small nod. "Thank you. I'm Nicole, by the way, and yes…if you really don't mind, I'd appreciate your help in locating Roscoe."

"Wouldn't have offered if I minded, and I'm Parker." He was about to say more when he noticed the headlights of an oncoming car. Yeah, definitely time to get out of the middle of the road. "Be careful," he warned as he opened his door. "And I'll see you in a few minutes."

"Miss Bradshaw!" Erin yelled from the back seat, taking advantage of the open car door. "It's us, Erin and Megan Lennox! You look very pretty and I'm glad we didn't run you over."

Nicole shielded her eyes and laughed. "Well, hello there, Erin and Megan. I'm glad you didn't run me over, too." Looking at Parker, she said, "You're their father, I take it?"

"I am."

"Nice to meet you, Parker-who-is-Megan-and-Erin's-father." She put on his coat, which was large enough on her frame to cover her wings, and zipped it to her chin. And darn if that halo of hers didn't droop a little more, increasing her adorable quotient by two. Or three.

"Likewise." Waving, he got into the driver's seat and buckled his seat belt, his interest and curiosity about Nicole already sky-high, and said to his girls, "Okay, no harm and no foul. Let's get out of the road and into the school, before anything else crazy happens."

"Yeah. No more crazy stuff!" Megan said. "Just *fun* stuff!"

In a matter of seconds, the girls were once again talking about the play and the possibility of both of them being angels. As they did, Parker watched Nicole cross to the other side of the street without incident and, even through his closed window, could hear her shouting "Roscoe!"

He grinned at the sight of a disheveled angel searching for her dog, and hoping she'd find him quickly, he turned off the car's emergency lights and veered into the proper lane. Less than a minute later, they were in the elementary school's parking lot. The girls were chattering in their normal manner as they left the car, and Parker tossed in a teasing comment or two.

But his thoughts were wholly focused on Nicole Bradshaw and the sizzle of electricity that had sped through his bloodstream as they talked, as he took in her crooked halo and—to him, anyway—ethereal features. He recognized the sizzle well enough, even though years had passed since he'd last experienced the sensation.

Because until just a few minutes ago, Bridget was

the only other woman Parker had ever looked at and felt that same pop of awareness, of innate chemistry and bone-deep attraction. It happened on the very first day he set eyes on Bridget Delaney, later to become Bridget Lennox, and every precious day they had together thereafter.

She was the woman he'd loved with every part of his heart and soul. The woman he'd had every intention of creating a long life and growing old with. The woman he still missed and longed for on a consistent, if not daily, basis. His daughters' mother. His wife. His Bridget.

Frankly, Parker did not know what to think of having the same—and up until now, unique—initial response to Nicole that he'd had with Bridget. But he sure as hell planned on exploring that reaction and discovering if lightning really could strike twice.

Chapter Two

Gosh darn it, where was that dog? Nicole swallowed the thick lump of fear in her throat and called out, "Roscoe! Come here, boy! Want a treat? Here, Roscoe!"

Nothing. Not a bark or a whine or a yelp of happiness.

Trudging forward, her eyes peeled as she yelled Roscoe's name every few feet, Nicole silently admitted that bringing her dog had been an error in judgment. Oh, he'd done well at the other school events she'd taken him to—a few ball games last spring, right after accepting the music teacher position, and the outdoor fair last month—and he loved children, but she should've known better. Her dog had a *serious* case of wanderlust.

He loved nothing better than running off to explore

and always took any chance given to escape. Due to this tendency, Nicole had learned to remain vigilant when she had Roscoe out of the house or her fenced-in backyard. Typically, she could keep his high-energy excitement under control. Tonight, in fact, was the first time in a long while that he'd managed to break free.

And no doubt about it, his getaway was her fault.

They had gone for a quick walk and had returned to the school about fifteen minutes before the tryouts were supposed to start, and no, she had not been paying close enough attention. They were in the auditorium, and she'd just finagled those stupid costume horns on Roscoe's head. At the exact second she unclipped his leash, the janitor cracked open the outside door. The dog instantly lunged forward, out of her grasp and racing with the wind.

So here she was, anxiously searching for her dog while dressed as an angel, which made her decision to bring Roscoe tonight seem naive. The idea of doing so hadn't even occurred to her until yesterday, and when she checked in with the school's principal this morning—who'd met the happy-and-affectionate Roscoe several times—he'd given his consent.

She'd hoped the sight of her large, funny-looking mixed-breed mutt, with stuffed reindeer horns on his head, would make the kids laugh, helping them to relax and have fun. And if all had actually gone as planned, his presence would've provided Nicole with a much-needed surge of confidence and eased her nerves. Mainly because she hadn't quite found her place in

Steamboat Springs yet, or solid footing as the elementary school's new music teacher.

The position became available only when the prior music teacher, Mrs. Engle, retired after forty years of devoted service. Everyone—the other teachers, the students and the parents—adored Mrs. Engle, and stepping into such beloved shoes was not a simple task. Especially since Mrs. Engle had always been in charge of the school's music and drama productions.

A responsibility that now fell on Nicole's shoulders, which was the primary cause for her anxiety. Oh, she'd directed many a recital in the past, while working and living in a suburb of Denver, and would do so again here without blinking an eye. But she'd never taken on the performance of an actual drama, and this one didn't include so much as a note of music. To add to her nerves, she'd chosen to skip the school's traditional presentation of the nativity story in favor of a lovely fairy-tale take on Charles Dickens's *A Christmas Carol.*

The kids didn't know this yet, and since she'd heard a few of her students talking about how they wanted to play Mary, one of the three Wise Men or an angel, she worried they would be disappointed when they learned the roles now up for grabs were fairy-tale characters such as Rumpelstiltskin in place of Ebenezer Scrooge and Pinocchio for Bob Cratchit.

Or they might love the change. Unfortunately, since she wasn't in the auditorium—where, at this moment, children and parents were waiting for her, likely impatient and wondering if they were wasting their time by sticking around—she wouldn't know one way or the other until she found her darned dog. And who knew how long that would take?

Nicole hollered Roscoe's name again, and then again. Still nothing. Wrapping her arms around herself, she shivered and tried to think rationally. Or, she supposed, like a dog.

Okay. Knowing Roscoe's proclivity for attention, he could have already made friends with a family who lived in one of these houses, and could now be curled up—exhausted from his mad dash—on someone's kitchen floor. Oh, Lord. She prayed that was the case. Because the possibility, however remote, of her dog being safe and sound in someone's home alleviated the sharpest edge of her fears. Roscoe's dog tags had all of the information anyone would require to locate her, including her name, the veterinarian's and their individual phone numbers.

Sticking her hands into the pockets of the coat Parker had lent her—the act of an honest-to-God gentleman, by the way—Nicole shivered again and squinted through the snow, which was now falling at a brisker pace. Even with the glow of the streetlights and the houses' porch lights, the curtain of white made it difficult to see very far in the distance.

"Roscoe!" she yelled as she continued her path along the sidewalk, every step taking her farther away from the school building. "Where are you, boy? Want a treat? Roscoe, come here!"

She stopped, listened and hoped. When her dog did not bound out of the shadows, she continued to walk and shout his name. The wind picked up speed and her halo slipped another inch to the side. Annoyed, she yanked the darned thing off her head and, very likely destroying it beyond repair, bent the halo in half and shoved it into Parker's coat pocket.

Another bad idea, dressing as an angel.

She'd done so for the same reason she decorated her dog's head: to help relax the kids and get them into the Christmas spirit, and the only other adult-size holiday costume the school had was for Santa Claus himself. While Nicole had nothing against the jolly old man, she had no desire to stick on a fake beard or wear that many layers of clothing.

Or, well, to be fully honest, the stuffed belly pillow had been what really put her off. Her deepest desire was to become pregnant, and the thought of seeing her stomach big and round due to a freaking pillow and not the baby she so yearned for had almost brought her to tears. Reason enough, right there, to go with the angel costume.

Another type of shiver—one of longing and antici-pation—rippled through Nicole's body. Had the proce-dure worked? Was she, even now, pregnant? Too soon to know, of course, as it had been only three days since her visit to the Denver fertility clinic for her fourth— and please, Lord, her final—attempt. Though, if she didn't conceive this month, she'd try again. And she'd keep on trying until she ran out of her harvested eggs, funds or hope.

Whichever of the three came first, but more likely than not, the first.

A year ago, her doctor had hesitantly given her the

go-ahead for one round of fertility injections, before her already-compromised ovarian function ceased to exist. It had worked, but she had only a limited number of eggs to work with, which meant she had a limited amount of time to conceive. But she wasn't about to give up unless she had no other choice.

History had taught her the importance of always moving toward her goals and doing whatever she could to fulfill her wants *today*. Because tomorrow or next month or two years down the road could be too late. Life offered zero guarantees. Which was why she had gone through a round of fertility injections a year ago, despite the concerns for her health, for the possible danger of the increased hormone levels raising her risk for recurrence.

Risk versus reward. The reward, naturally, was a baby.

And oh, how she yearned to become a mother. Not only was she ready for the commitment, but with everything she'd gone through and the fears she'd faced head-on, she was a stronger woman now than ever before. She loved life. She loved *her* life.

All she needed to make the world—*her* world—complete was her child.

Shaking her head to clear her thoughts, Nicole turned to walk in the opposite direction, having no idea which way Roscoe had lumbered off. As far as she knew, if he wasn't safely ensconced in someone's house or still running and exploring, he might have returned to the school and was now wandering the parking lot in search of treats, kids to play with and hands to stroke his back. Roscoe soaked in love with the absorbency of a sponge.

In her hurry, she pivoted so fast that she came close to barging into another body—a strong, tall body that belonged to none other than Parker Lennox, the handsome blue-eyed, sandy-blond widower all the teachers raved about—and her feet, which were encased in slippery-soled flats, skidded on the snowy concrete, causing her to lose her balance and topple backward.

Mere seconds before her angel-gowned behind smacked the hard, frozen ground for the second time in less than thirty minutes, Parker grabbed her by the arms and yanked her upright. The sudden change in momentum sent her tumbling forward, directly into his solid—oh, wow, *very* solid—chest. Strong arms came around her, holding her steady.

Security and well-being stole in, quickly followed by a strange, dizzying sensation of déjà vu. If she believed in such things, she might think that some small part of her, by his touch alone, recognized this man and had, in fact, been waiting for him to arrive in her life. To do what? Make all her dreams come true and supply her with a happily-ever-after ending?

Ha. Now, *that* would be a fairy tale fit for the stage.

"Tell me," Parker said, his arms still around her and his voice somewhat amused, "are one-after-another collisions typical for you, Miss Bradshaw? Or am I a special case?"

"Nicole, please." Embarrassment warmed her cheeks, from those out-there, happily-ever-after thoughts. She pulled free from his grasp to stand on her own, but they were still a little too close for comfort. *Her* comfort. Carefully retreating a few feet, she said, "And it seems you must be a special case, as no, I'm not normally so clumsy."

"Hmm," he said, still sounding amused. "I don't believe I've knocked a woman off her feet in thirty-plus years, and now it's happened twice in one night. Should I be flattered or concerned enough for your safety that I keep a certain distance between us?"

Laughing, she scanned the area for Roscoe and tried to ignore the attraction sizzling in her blood. Hard to do, especially when combined with the security, the stability, she'd experienced while in his arms. Something she absolutely could have used those many days and weeks she'd spent in the hospital, when—between the horrors of chemotherapy and several surgeries—she feared that fate would not grant her another tomorrow, let alone a baby.

Fortunately, she had survived. And four years later, she remained blissfully healthy.

"Don't take this the wrong way," she said in response to Parker's question, "but you shouldn't feel flattered or concerned. I've simply had one of those days. We all have them."

"That we do." Tucking his arm into hers, as if he'd done so on numerous occasions in the past, he said, "But since today is one of those days for you, I will feel significantly better if I do everything in my power to see that you don't fall down again."

Nicole could have yanked her arm free and insisted she was completely able to walk without his assistance—which, of course, she was—but this time, instead of being smacked over the head with déjà vu, all she felt, from the tips of her toes to the top of her now halo-free head, was the safe, steady balance that Parker seemed to embody. And in a snap, her anxiety over her missing dog and being late at the school diminished to a much more manageable level.

So she allowed their arms to remain linked and said, "I suppose that's fair. But if we don't find Roscoe soon, I should probably go back to the school and…" Trailing off, she sighed. She did not want to return to the auditorium without her dog. "I just hope we find him soon."

"Then that's what we'll do," Parker said with confidence. "Where have you looked?"

"The way I just came. But I didn't knock on doors or look in backyards. I probably should have, but I thought he'd come when he heard my voice." He normally did, even if it was only to show himself and take off running again. Darn it! She *needed* to find Roscoe.

That silly, overgrown dog was her best friend and her sanctuary. Now and when she'd fought for her life. Her parents and her brother had held her hand and helped in every way they could have back then, but Roscoe was the only soul she'd shared her worst fears with.

"Let's go the other way past the school," Parker said, leading them in that direction. "Don't worry. He's out here somewhere, and between his moose-like size and…uh…that pair of horns on his head, he'll be hard to miss. Those were horns, right?"

"Yeah. Dumb idea, dressing him like a reindeer."

Parker chuckled. "Maybe that's why he ran away, out of humiliation."

"Oh, not hardly. I used to…" Pausing, she swallowed the words she'd almost said, that she used to buy matching bandannas for her head and his neck, when she'd lost her hair and didn't feel like wearing a wig. "He doesn't mind being dressed in…anything. I'm more worried he might scare whomever he comes across, since it's dark and hard to identify that he's a dog."

"Ah. Gotcha. What breed is he, by the way? I didn't get a good enough look to tell."

"Who knows?" she said with a forced laugh. "He's a Heinz 57."

"So he could be part moose," Parker said. And while she couldn't see his face, she could imagine his grin without too much trouble. "And you're from Denver? I'm guessing, based on the reason most people move here, that you're a skier?"

Nicole yelled for Roscoe before responding. "I can ski, but I'd prefer not to. Much to the dismay of my family, who are all avid skiers. My brother, Ryan, relocated here several years ago because of the skiing, and about six months later, my parents followed. They're all about the slopes, so you were right in a way, but I moved here to be close to family."

"I see. Well, that's important."

"Yep. I…didn't have any real reason to stay in Denver and my family is one of those super-duper, annoyingly close types. Of course, I had to find a job here first, and since music teacher positions are relatively scarce—especially in smaller communities—I had to be patient."

The entire statement held 100 percent truth, but Nicole didn't share that the largest portion of her decision was due to wanting a baby. If that hope came to fruition, living near her parents and Ryan would be paramount. For support and love, yes, but also… Well, she'd already had cancer once. She could become ill again. A horrible consideration, but one she had to take seriously before bringing a child into this world. Because if fate dealt her such a vicious blow a second time, and she didn't survive, her parents would become her child's guardian.

And if that happened? Living here would ensure that her son or daughter wouldn't have to move to a new city, change schools or make new friends in the midst of his or her grief. It was the best she could do in controlling an otherwise-uncontrollable situation.

Oh, no way in hell was she planning on dying. Nicole was planning on living to the ripe old age of one hundred. Or longer! But she couldn't have a baby without considering every possibility. Even the bad ones that you never wanted to think about or prepare for.

Today, though, she was healthy. Strong. *Happy.* And she might already be pregnant! All she needed in this minute was to find her dog, get herself to the school and do her job, and then wait on pins and needles for ten or so days until she could take a pregnancy test.

"Family is everything," Parker said quietly, interrupting her thoughts. "My parents retired to Florida a while back, and my sister lived in California for quite some time. She lives here now, though. Happily married with a couple of kids. Twins."

"My brother was recently married, but they don't have any kids yet." They probably would soon, though, and then Nicole would be an aunt. She'd love and spoil her niece or nephew, without doubt, and she adored her new sister-in-law. Andi was sweet and funny and perfect for Ryan. Even so, Nicole couldn't deny that a pang of jealousy swirled in with the rest. "But wow, twins," she said, forcing herself to continue the conversation. "That seems crazy and wonderful, all at once. Boys or girls? And are they identical or fraternal?"

"One boy, one girl, so that means they're fraternal. They're toddlers, so my sister and brother-in-law—their names are Daisy and Reid—have their hands full. Big-time." Parker laughed and then, raising his voice, called out for Roscoe. "But yeah," he said a minute later, "it's always good to have family nearby. Makes the difficulties of life easier."

Did it ever. Nicole sighed in disappointment when her dog failed to appear and in, well, another shot of envy. "Two babies, one of each, at the same time," she said. "How perfect is that? If you don't mind me asking, what are their names?"

"Why would I mind? The twins are Charlotte and Alexander. My girls are like little mothers whenever we're all together. It's kind of great to see, actually."

"I bet it is." She took a turn hollering for her absentee dog, and again, no sound or sight of the furry, lovable canine followed. Emotion she'd so far managed to repress kicked in good and hard, and she inhaled a large breath in an attempt to calm down before breaking into tears in front of a man whom, while kind and charming, she did not really know.

The idea of crying in Parker's presence sent her tears scurrying for cover. Nicole disliked crying in front of anyone except for Roscoe. At first because the only time her tears seemed able to show themselves was when she was alone at home, with just her dog for company.

Now she thought this tendency had more to do with her intense desire to present a strong, calm visage to the world, no matter the circumstances. Doing so helped her feel less vulnerable to forces outside of her control, even though she knew full well that keeping her emotions under wraps wouldn't stop her from being hurt or becoming ill again.

"Roscoe! Come here, boy!" Parker's deep voice whipped into the night air, likely carrying much farther than hers could and startling her to renewed awareness. His hold on her arm tightened, and again, she felt that irresistible wash of comfort and absolute security.

"Thank you," she said to Parker, "for not running over me or my dog and for going above and beyond." Her hair was wet from the snow, her legs and feet were freezing, the wind stung her cheeks. But thanks to Parker's close proximity and his coat, the portion of her body from hips to shoulders remained toasty warm. "You didn't have to give me your coat or leave your kids to come out here and try to help find Roscoe. I... You've been very nice."

"You're welcome," he said. "But trust me, I'm

equally as glad I didn't mow you or your dog over, and helping is the right thing to do. My girls are fine. They're waiting with some friends, being watched over by plenty of adults. And frankly, what kind of man would I be if I allowed an angel's wings to freeze?"

"Well…still. You have to be frozen."

"Nah. I'm wearing a couple of layers, so I'm okay. Let's just focus on getting Roscoe back to you. Where he belongs."

By now, they'd just about reached the section of houses that stood directly across from the school, and Nicole considered calling a temporary halt to the search. For the sake of her job and the many kids and parents waiting. Yet, how could she give up when Roscoe was out here, somewhere in the dark, cold and maybe hurt—*oh*, she prayed, *don't let him be hurt*—all by himself? She couldn't. So that left her with one alternative.

"Can you do me a favor?" she asked, going with her gut. "I can't stop looking for him, but I also can't ignore that people are waiting for me in the auditorium. Could you let everyone know that I'll reschedule the tryouts for…oh, next week, I guess? Since today is Friday."

"Sure. I can do that for you, no problem," Parker said instantly, making her believe he was more than ready to give up the search even if she wasn't. Duh. Of course he was. The responsibility to locate her dog fell on her shoulders, not his. They barely knew each other.

"Thank you," she repeated. "I really appreciate—"

"If you want my opinion, though," Parker broke in, "I think you should come inside and change out of that costume into something warmer. When you're all set, we can continue the search by car. We'll be faster if we drive a loop around the entire area than if we keep walking."

Nicole blinked, surprised and warmed through and through by Parker's offer. "You don't have to. I mean, you've already done more than enough. But changing into my normal clothes is a great idea, so I can get my coat and return yours."

"Again, I wouldn't have offered unless it was something I wanted to do," Parker said as they started the trek across the street. Still arm in arm. "Besides which, my daughters will want to help. Actually, they'll insist. And let's face it—four pairs of eyes are far better than one."

"Okay, I accept," Nicole said after only the slightest of hesitations. If Parker wanted to lend a hand, then why argue? Especially since he was right. The more people on the lookout for Roscoe, the better chance she had of finding him tonight. "Redundant maybe, but thank you."

A soft, husky rumble of a laugh emerged from his chest. "I have never been thanked so often in such a short amount of time, but you're very welcome, Nicole. While the circumstances are less than ideal, I'm enjoying this—getting to know you—quite a bit."

Nicole's cheeks burned even hotter. It had been a while since a man's comments had made her blush. So long, she couldn't even remember the last occurrence. Of course, she hadn't dated seriously since before her illness and had dated only a few men after. One of whom could have become a long-term partner—she'd liked him enough for that to happen, at any rate—but once she told him that she was a cancer survivor, he disappeared into thin air.

As in, she had never heard from him again. Not a phone call or an email. Not even a cowardly text message. Evidently, her cancer confession had spooked the man and sent him running for the hills. She understood why, and it wasn't as if they'd dated for very long, but his vanishing act without so much as a goodbye hurt. It made her realize that most men would likely view her as damaged goods, and she did not need that label put on her. From anyone.

Easier to call a halt to dating altogether.

So she had, and until now, she hadn't really missed having a man in her life. But Parker—by virtue of his kind, considerate behavior and, okay, enormous sex appeal—had seemingly ignited her onetime yearning for love. A yearning that wouldn't do her any good at all. Unlike her deep desire for a baby, which she potentially—and with a lot of help—had the power to fulfill, wishing for a man to love her was completely useless.

She couldn't visit a clinic to get a man, now, could she?

The simplest and sanest explanation for Parker's attention boiled down to good manners and a normal inclination to help someone in need. Even if he was somewhat interested in her as a woman, he would change his mind the second he discovered her rocky medical history. Why wouldn't he? Not only was Parker a widower, but if what Nicole had heard was correct, his wife had died from the same disease that could have claimed her life: breast cancer.

Yeah. He'd run for the hills, too. And she wouldn't blame him.

So tonight, she'd accept his help and revel in his attention, and perhaps a friendship between them might develop. But no more than that. For his sake, his daughters' sakes and even for Nicole's. She might be pregnant. In a year's time, she might be a mother.

Therefore, despite her body's reactions to Parker and the slight—*very* slight—possibility of his interest in her, she had zero room in her life for anyone or anything else. Nicole's entire focus needed to remain on her good health, getting pregnant and becoming a mother.

Nothing else mattered. Nothing else *could* matter. Simple as that.

Chapter Three

The next morning, Parker and the girls were finishing their breakfast, and naturally, the topic of discussion was the night before. His daughters had already reenacted their version of "Daddy almost killing an angel who really turned out to be Miss Bradshaw, the best music teacher ever!" and had now moved on to their sadness that Roscoe hadn't been located.

Not that they hadn't tried. Once Nicole had promised those waiting in the auditorium that the tryouts would be rescheduled for next week, she changed out of her angel getup and into a pair of jeans and a sweatshirt. The four of them—Parker, Nicole, Erin and Megan—had then driven at a snail's pace the two blocks in each direction around the school.

They'd searched for over an hour, to no avail. And

Parker would've kept on searching, but without so much as a glimpse of the moose-size dog and the difficulty of seeing much of anything in the dark, Nicole insisted that they'd done enough for the night. He hated giving up. He hated the tears he heard in her voice when he dropped her off at her car, back at the school, and they said their goodbyes. But in the end, it was her dog and her choice.

Though, despite her assurances that she was going home, he had an inkling that she'd continued looking on her own and was mainly set on letting him off the hook. Without doubt, his preference was to stay with Nicole and help, but he didn't argue. Again—her dog, her choice. Besides which, he had the sense that she needed to cry and wouldn't do so in front of him or his daughters. None of this stopped him from taking one more trip around the school, just in case Roscoe was ready to be found, before he and the girls went home.

If Nicole hadn't had any better luck once they parted ways, he knew her plan was to phone the various animal shelters the second they opened today. Perhaps she'd already had good news and would shortly be reunited with her dog. He hoped so.

As if reading his mind, Megan said, "Do you think Miss Bradshaw found Roscoe yet?"

"I don't know, honey. But it would be really great if she has."

"We should find out, Daddy," Erin said. "You should call her and ask. Because if she hasn't, we can draw posters and put them up all over, so people know to watch for him."

It wasn't the worst idea Parker had ever heard. Actually, it was a damn good one. He particularly liked the "you should call her" portion of Erin's suggestion. Supposing, of course, Nicole's phone number was listed. "You know, I like that plan, kiddo," he said to Erin. "Why don't you two grab the art supplies and start on the posters now? That way, if Roscoe hasn't been found, we save a little time. And I'll see if I can get a hold of your music teacher."

"Okay, Daddy!" Erin shot to a stand. "Come on, Megan! Let's get the markers and glue and glitter and... Oh, but we don't have any pictures of Roscoe. We don't really know what he looks like, just that he's big and brown, so how can we make signs for people to find him?"

"We can use stickers!" Megan said. "We have lots and lots of puppy dog stickers."

"But we don't know if Roscoe looks like any of the dogs on those stickers." Erin's shoulders slumped in defeat. "This won't work without any pictures of Roscoe."

"Sure it will," Parker said, automatically offering encouragement. "Think about the problem for a minute. It's true that we don't have any photos of Roscoe, but someone else likely has a ton of pictures. Who might that person be?"

"Miss Bradshaw," Erin and Megan said at the same time.

"That's right. And I'm sure she'll let us pick the best one to use." Assuming she hadn't already located her missing pooch. "Then we can make however many copies of it we need and glue them to the signs. Just remember to leave a big enough space in the middle when you're making them, and we'll be all set. Do you think that will work?"

"Yes!" Megan jumped to her feet and tugged her sister's arm. "Let's go get everything and make the best dog signs ever, Erin. For Miss Bradshaw, so she isn't sad anymore."

It didn't surprise Parker that Megan had tuned in to Nicole's sadness last night or that she wanted to help alleviate that sadness. Both of his daughters tended to be very aware of the people around them and their moods. Probably due to the last weeks of their mother's life, when the house had been filled with friends and family wanting to say their goodbyes. And while Megan's personal recollections of her mother were very sparse—almost, sadly, nonexistent—that didn't mean the experience itself hadn't carved into her heart, her soul, and etched an indelible mark.

Some moments, some types of pain, were unforgettable. No matter the age.

Parker repressed a sigh and waited for the girls to climb the steps to retrieve the art supplies from the upstairs hall closet before powering on his laptop. It didn't take long to ascertain that Nicole's number was not listed or, perhaps, that her number was so new it had yet to make it to the online directories. There were several other Bradshaws, though, and while Nicole hadn't mentioned her parents' first names, she had identified her brother as Ryan.

And thankfully, within the half-dozen Bradshaws that were listed, there was only one Ryan. So, hoping he didn't come off as a crazy stalker, Parker dialed the number and crossed his fingers that Ryan was home. And that he'd either give Parker his sister's phone number—doubtful, because if some stranger contacted Parker looking for Daisy, no way, no how would he give out her personal information—or be willing to pass on a message to Nicole.

The man answered almost instantly, and after he got over his surprise and had asked several pointed questions, he promised to contact Nicole on Parker's behalf. Fifteen minutes later, with the girls avidly focused on their Find this Dog! Please! posters, Parker's phone rang.

It was Nicole. Anticipation of hearing her voice, of possibly seeing her today, sent his pulse into overdrive and his stomach into a series of wicked fast, hard somersaults. Responses that also reminded him of the early days with Bridget, when she'd consumed his thoughts and he'd gathered every strand of his young man's courage to ask her out for a date.

Yeah, he liked Nicole. A lot, if his body's reactions were anything to go by—and of course, they were. He'd acted on those instincts with Bridget.

So why wouldn't he act on them now?

Parker inhaled a stabilizing breath, grinned at his daughters, who were watching him with expectant, eager eyes, and, doing his level best to keep his voice at an even keel, picked up and answered his phone. To talk to the woman he could not get out of his head.

Why, oh, why had she agreed to let Parker and his daughters come over? Nicole tugged the window's curtain to the side and peeked out, anxious to start searching for Roscoe. When she contacted the shelters an hour ago, none of them had any dogs that even remotely resembled him. Now at least they had her information. So if he was brought in and had somehow lost his dog tags, she'd be notified. But oh, was she disappointed.

All she could do was get back on the street and scour every nook and cranny. She'd start at the school, follow the same path they had last night and then branch out in a wider circle, asking anyone she came across if they'd seen Roscoe. Certainly, she'd have better luck today.

Ready to get moving, Nicole gathered her coat, gloves and the picture of Roscoe she'd printed from her computer to show people and put them in a neat pile near the front door before returning to her post at the window.

When Ryan had phoned, his initial questions were about her—how was she, how had Roscoe gotten loose?—and then, after he'd expressed his sorrow and concern, he reminded her that he was heading to Rhode Island for a week to spend time with Andi's family, but offered to stay and help. She appreciated her brother's willingness to do so but told him he absolutely shouldn't alter his plans. And that was when he finally gave her Parker's message.

As he repeated the conversation he'd had with Parker, electricity and anticipation had zinged through her blood in a potent reminder of her attraction. She wasn't ashamed to admit that the zing itself had felt nice. Thrilling and liberating and so wonderfully normal. It was that zing, that feeling of normalcy, that led her to return Parker's call immediately, rather than the more sensible approach of waiting until after she'd put in a few hours searching for her dog.

The sound of his voice, calm, steady and confident, somehow strengthened her flagging hope. He'd asked about Roscoe, naturally, and if she'd made any headway with the shelters. She could hear Megan and Erin in the background, their voices almost a high-pitched squeal in their enthusiasm, begging Parker to ask Nicole their questions.

He did, in a serious manner and one after another, pass on their queries, which consisted of: "How old is Roscoe?" "Is his hair light, medium or dark brown?" "What is his favorite dog treat?" And finally, "What color are Roscoe's eyes?"

Nicole had given the girls the same information in the car last night, but she answered the questions again in a mix of curiosity, appreciation and good humor. They were sweet kids who obviously wanted to help bring Roscoe home. So Parker's query if they could stop by and lend their services for the next round of searching didn't surprise her in the least. Even as she thought the words *Thank you, but no*, what came out of her mouth was "Yes, if you're sure."

Probably, Parker's reason for extending his hand yet again had more to do with his daughters' excitement than it did from any true desire of his own. And that was fine. It, in fact, mirrored her primary reason for accepting their assistance. How could she let down two little girls whose hearts were in the right place? She couldn't. Add in the zing and the intoxicating quality of his voice, and she didn't even *want* to decline.

But waiting around for them to arrive while her dog was still missing and running loose somewhere was beginning to take a heavy toll.

Sickness lurched in her stomach, kicking her hard and solidifying into a seemingly impenetrable mass, at the prospect that perhaps Roscoe wasn't running loose. Because he wasn't able to. Because he'd been hit by a car and was hurt or... No. Her dog was smart, agile and fast. She refused to go to worst-case scenarios. He hadn't even been missing twenty-four hours yet.

Glancing through the window a second time and still not seeing any sign of Parker and his daughters, Nicole sighed in pent-up frustration and worry. She'd give them ten more minutes before sending Parker a text with her apologies and the explanation that she couldn't wait any longer. Yes, Erin and Megan would be disappointed, but they were intelligent and compassionate little girls. They would understand and she'd make it up to them somehow.

For the next seven and a half minutes, Nicole paced her sparsely furnished living room and tried to direct her thoughts away from Roscoe's whereabouts. She'd sold or gotten rid of most of her secondhand furniture when she moved to Steamboat Springs from Denver, knowing she would live with her parents until she found a house to purchase. She had done so in the middle of the summer and had settled in here only about a month ago. As of yet, she hadn't finished replacing all she'd sold, preferring to go slowly in order to enjoy the process.

Her house, built in the style of a Craftsman bungalow, was a spectacular deal. The owners were relocating and had been motivated to sell fast at a below-market price; otherwise she likely would've had to pass. And that would've been a shame, as the second she walked through the front door, she had fallen completely in love.

Coming in at close to 1,700 finished square feet, the house was larger than what Nicole had been looking for, and the lowered sale price, while a great bargain, still pushed hard at the limit of her budget. But her gut had insisted she'd found her home. She trusted that instinct and, in the end, swallowed her nerves and took the plunge.

The exterior of the house featured dark blue siding with a sturdy gray brick foundation and, to her delight, a lovely screened-in front porch where she could sit and drink her tea before getting ready for work. And the interior of the house was perfect.

Every inch of the living space existed on the first floor and included three bedrooms, a cozy dining room that sat directly next to the eat-in kitchen, a laundry nook that more than suited Nicole's needs, a spacious living room and two full bathrooms. In addition, the house boasted a second floor that had a single room, which was large but unfinished. The prior homeowners, before having to relocate, had planned on turning the upstairs room into their master bedroom.

They never had, and Nicole doubted she'd ever go

to the trouble. She didn't require the extra living space and it worked well for storage. Plus, when the home was originally built, the second floor hadn't even been wired for electricity. Why go to the hassle and expense for an unnecessary addition, especially when she had yet to finish filling the rooms she did use?

At the moment, the only furniture in the living room was the pair of comfy, overstuffed chairs Nicole had bought at a going-out-of-business sale, a stand-up lamp she'd shoved in the corner and her television. The lamp wasn't even hers, as she'd borrowed it from her parents. Before Roscoe's getaway, her plans for today had included furniture shopping.

She'd hoped to find a sofa and maybe even a couple of end tables or, if she had no luck there, a few knick-knacks for the brick fireplace's mantel. A vase or—

The slam of a car door, followed quickly by another, woke her from her musings. They were here. Thank God! Nicole went to the front door and opened it without waiting for a knock or the doorbell to ring. She was instantly greeted with three voices—that of two little girls, still talking excitedly, as well as their father's deep, resonating tone—and out of nowhere, her heart picked up an extra beat and what felt like a million goose bumps coated her skin.

What a gorgeous family these three made. The man—tall and lean, sexy and strong, with a warm smile in his sky blue eyes and on his rugged face—and those two adorable little girls by his side. Erin, with her golden-highlighted coppery-red hair gleaming in the morning sun and her pixie-like features—her softly pointed chin, small turned-up nose and finely etched cheekbones—and Megan, whose hair fell to her slim shoulders in a swoop of silky pale gold, with her expressive, friendly brown eyes and eager, happy-to-be-me grin.

Yes. They were a striking trio, and as they approached the front porch, Nicole wondered about the girls' mother. She must have been a stunning woman. Red haired, possibly, like Erin, and almost certainly brown eyed, like both of her daughters. And Nicole then thought of the illness that had taken this mystery woman's life, the illness she herself had fought with such vehemence, and her heart went out to these two little girls. To Parker.

Not only for the crushing, devastating loss of a mother and wife, but for the unbelievable hell that came before. The consuming fear when the diagnosis was first delivered, the slender strands of hope that couldn't truly be grasped onto because of the overriding terror, the misery—oh, the horrible, horrible misery—of chemotherapy. Losing her hair, losing her identity, trying to have a positive attitude and keep it all together for her girls, for her husband, for herself.

Nicole didn't have to imagine the terror or the hard-to-find hope or the god-awful misery. She was well acquainted with how it felt to watch your hair fall out, to look in the mirror and not recognize your own reflection, and to, well, to feel so ill that at times the possibility of losing the battle, of dying, came as almost a salve to the soul. Those struggles, those emotions, those realities she had experienced and would never, for the rest of her life, forget.

But she did not have children or a husband who had so needed her to survive, who depended on her and loved her, to worry about. To fear for or to try to remain strong for. Nicole could not put herself fully in this woman's shoes, could not fathom how much courage and strength she'd been forced to find or the deep, desperate sorrow she must have felt when she knew that death was coming and that she couldn't do anything but wait for the end.

Yes, Nicole had worried for her parents and her brother, and yes, she'd absolutely attempted to remain resilient and optimistic for their benefit, if not her own. And that wasn't nothing. But it wasn't the same, either. Did not, could not, hold an intensity equal to looking at your cherished children and hating the fact that you wouldn't be there for them as they grew.

The weight of unshed tears appeared behind Nicole's eyes. She pushed them down deep and forced the depressing thoughts into submission. They'd be there, she knew, to later pick apart and once again consider everything she had already considered so many times: the wisdom of purposely attempting to have a child without a husband in the wings ready to take over if her life ended, whether by a stupid accident of fate or the recurrence of her deadliest and most feared enemy.

Except now, along with the scary what-ifs—*if* she became pregnant, *if* she became ill again, *if* she didn't survive—she would see this family in her mind's eye. She would think of Parker and Erin and Megan, and the undeniable facts of all they must have gone through and how very much they'd lost. And while she might already be pregnant, she'd have no choice but to once more weigh the risks against the benefits of her choice and decide if that balance had changed. If she was pregnant, she'd joyously move forward with hope and commitment. But if her fourth procedure had failed as the first three had, then yes, she'd reconsider everything from top to bottom with a different, more defined view and see where she landed.

She doubted she would change her mind, but she recognized that ignoring the weight on her heart, the stark reality of these two little girls growing up without their mother, would prove impossible. She had thought about them before, what they had experienced, when she'd first learned of their mother's passing from one of the other teachers, but now that she'd spent time with Erin and Megan outside of the classroom, her reaction to that basic knowledge had become more intense.

But those thoughts weren't for now. She had a dog to find and two beautiful little girls plus one handsome daddy to welcome into her home. So, centering every ounce of her energy on the present, she smiled at her guests, who had just reached the front porch, and said, "Hey there, guys! I'm glad you're here. Come on in and we'll—"

"Hi, Miss Bradshaw!" Erin said. "We're glad we're here, too. And you'll never guess what we did! We brought you a surprise. To help us find Roscoe."

"Oh?" She took a closer look at Parker and finally noticed a stack of large drawings, bright and colorful with stickers and glitter, in his grasp. Blinking, she read the lettering on the topmost drawing and she saw what these precious girls had done for her. And her heart melted into a pile of sticky goo. "You girls are amazing," she said. "Thank you."

"You're welcome," Erin said. "And it was my idea."

"But we both worked really hard," Megan added. "Because we want Roscoe to come home so you won't be sad and he'll be safe. We didn't have any pictures of him, but Daddy said we could probably get one from you and that we should just leave a big space in the middle."

"I have plenty of pictures, for sure," Nicole said, still surprised. Still tingly. And feeling about as fortunate and blessed as a woman with a missing dog could. "And I already have one picked out that I was going to use to show people. So, I'll just print more."

"Or make some copies! Daddy said that, too, and—"

"Take a breath, Megan," Parker said, widening his smile. He winked at Nicole and now her gooey heart did the impossible. It fluttered. "I know you're excited and want to show Miss Bradshaw the signs you worked so hard on, but why don't we go inside first?"

Nicole returned his smile but not his wink, and opening the door another margin, she waited for all three to enter. Once they had, the girls kneeled to take off their snowy boots without being asked, and Parker handed her the stack of signs so he could do the same. Their fingers touched, for a brief, hardly there second, and the *zing* returned. Along with that punch—more of a wallop, really—of intrinsic recognition and connection. To this man.

Without warning, something—hope, maybe—that she'd buried in a locked, steel alloy box broke free and blossomed into being. She'd given up on the idea of love, of being lucky enough to find the right man to cherish and who would cherish her in return, to build a life with. But here it was again, as bright and shiny as a new penny. And far too appealing.

What if this recognition and connection and tingly awareness she felt toward Parker could actually become the love she never thought she'd have? Based on her past and what she knew of his, a bona fide miracle would have to occur. And really, how many miracles could a woman expect to have? She'd already been graced with her life, becoming healthy again, and she was, even now, doing everything in her power to become pregnant, which would absolutely count as a second miracle. There was Roscoe, too. Finding him would be number three.

Three miracles seemed greedy enough. How could she possibly hope for a fourth?

"I know it has to be difficult, but try not to worry too much, Nicole," Parker said quietly, retrieving the signs from her grasp and then handing them to his daughters. They took them and rushed into the living room. "Focus on Roscoe and how he is very likely holed up somewhere safe and sound, and that he'll be back home by the end of the day."

"Good advice and that's what I keep telling myself," she said, trying to sound upbeat. "I'm just worried, I guess. I don't know what I would do without him. He's my best friend and an important part of my family. That might seem weird to say, but it's true."

"Not weird. I'd call it normal and expected. I've never had a dog, but my sister has a canine member of her family." He nodded toward his daughters, who were in the process of laying the posters side by side on the living room floor. "She's a sweet dog—feisty but sweet. Jinx adores kids, and the girls love her. It was hard on them when Daisy and Jinx moved out."

Toddler twins, a sweet and feisty dog and a loving husband. Parker's sister seemed to have it all. Some women really were blessed with everything. And that was fine. Good, even. Nicole did not need *everything* to be content and satisfied with all she *did* have. She wouldn't refuse more, but who would? She just didn't *require* more.

"I'm sure it was difficult," she said. "How long did your sister live with you?"

"Oh. For a while. She took care of Erin and Megan when I was in the hospital." A shadow crossed Parker's features, which he quickly masked with a smile. "My point is, I have a small idea of what you're going through, even though the circumstances are different."

"Right. Of course. I didn't mean to suggest that you didn't." She was curious about why he had been in the hospital and for how long, but didn't ask. Even if the girls weren't within hearing distance, it wasn't her business. She *hated* talking about her illness, treatment and recovery. The entire topic made her uncomfortable. "We…uh…should get moving. I'll print off more pictures of Roscoe so the girls can finish their amazing posters, and then we'll head out."

"Perfect," Parker said, moving toward his daughters. By now, they were sitting on the floor in front of their handiwork, waiting about as patiently as two kids could. "I was thinking we might want to stop by Fosters Bar and Grill when we're ready for a break. They get a lot of business, and my sister is married to one of the Fosters. I'm sure they'd hang one for us."

She followed Parker's path and stopped near the trio. "That would be great," she said. "Thank you. And you guys wait here. I'll be right back with those pictures. We need eight?"

"We have eight posters, so yes, please!" Erin said.

Megan worried her lower lip with her teeth. "I hope we left big enough spaces."

"We did," Erin said, "but we can cut the pictures smaller if we need to."

"So long as we don't cut off part of Roscoe's face," Megan said. "Because we can't redo the posters. We left all of our art supplies at home, and we'd have to go back."

"Girls, we won't have to redo anything," Parker said. "You left plenty of room."

Nicole smiled at their chatter and went to the bedroom she used as an office. Quickly, because she was ready to search for her dog, she found the correct picture of Roscoe on her laptop and set it to print eight copies. Her brain returned to Parker's statement about being in the hospital. Had he been sick or was there an accident or...?

Again, she reminded herself that whatever the cause of his hospital stay, it wasn't her business. Besides which, if Parker wanted her to know more, he'd tell her on his own. If he was anything like her, and it was a topic that made him uncomfortable, he wouldn't. And since she had firsthand experience in the discomfort of unwanted questions, she would never put another person through the same misery. But that didn't stop her curiosity or her concern.

She hoped that whatever had happened was over and done with and well in the past.

A sigh emerged as the eighth sheet of paper spit from the printer. Today, she didn't have to think about anything except for finding Roscoe, and she wouldn't have to answer any of those hated questions. Parker did not know she was a breast cancer survivor. To him, she was just his daughters' music teacher who had lost her dog. Nothing more, nothing less.

Better all the way around to keep it that way.

Chapter Four

Three hours of searching and putting up the Find This Dog, Please! posters had resulted in grumbling bellies, sore legs, and sadly, hadn't yet brought them any closer to locating the angel's missing dog. As much as Parker hated to call a time-out, one was needed. Not only for Erin and Megan, but also for Nicole. She was dragging just as much as his girls.

Probably more, actually, if her heartbroken state was taken into consideration.

So, he'd slowly worked their path toward Fosters Bar and Grill, and once they were on the same block as the restaurant, he said, "Time for a break. Let's get some food and warm up, drop off this last poster, and then give it a couple more hours. What do you say?"

He expected Nicole to urge him and the girls to do

as he suggested, but to insist that she would keep going and meet back up with them later. Or worse, that she'd thank them politely for their assistance, but say that they had done enough and should go home. The idea of stopping, even for a necessary recharge, wouldn't sit well with her determination to bring Roscoe home.

The woman had a steel backbone and the seeming ability to push herself for however long it took to reach a desired goal. Admirable traits that Parker respected, but whether right or wrong, he had the gut-deep desire to see to her well-being. Allowing her to continue without rest and sustenance, a chance to regroup and find some level of peace again, went against that desire.

So he would insist, if necessary. He was as determined as she.

Surprisingly, she simply nodded and said, "A break sounds good."

Both pleased and concerned she'd agreed so easily, he led the way to the restaurant and held open the door while his daughters and Nicole stepped inside. There were a few tables available, so he chose one on the other side of the room, farthest from the bar and near a window. A quick scan showed the middle Foster brother, Dylan, behind the bar; the matriarch of the Foster clan, Margaret, and the only daughter, Haley, waiting tables. There was another bartender and waitress also working, but neither were members of the Foster family.

There was always at least one Foster present at the restaurant, as well as the sporting goods store, which was another family-owned business. Unusual for three family members to be working at the same time in the middle of the day, but it was the start of the busy winter season for Steamboat Springs. Likely, someone had called in sick today or the restaurant wasn't yet fully staffed for the season. Either way, he was pleased. The Fosters were good people.

And he didn't only think that because his sister was married to Reid, who happened to be his best friend. The Fosters were Parker's family long before it became official.

"I want chicken strips and french fries," Erin said as soon as they were all seated. They ate here often, so the girls rarely looked at the menu. "And strawberry lemonade."

"I think we can handle that," Parker said. "What about you, Megan?"

"Um. I don't know yet. What are you getting, Miss Bradshaw?"

Nicole leaned back in her chair and let out a long breath, closed her eyes for a millisecond and then said, "I haven't lived here that long and I've never eaten here before, Megan, so I'll need your help in deciding. What do you usually get? What do you never get?"

Megan's eyes rounded. "You've never been here before? We're here all the time."

Great. Now it sounded as if Parker never cooked. He did. Pancakes were his specialty. "Everything is good here, Nicole, and, kiddo…I wouldn't say we're here all the time. More like once a week. Sometimes, twice, if we have a lot going on after school."

"We were here three times last week, Daddy," Erin

said, her tone playful. "Remember? But it's okay. We like eating here, and then we don't have to clean dishes after dinner."

Nicole laughed, and the glow in her gaze returned. "I'd say the phrase 'all the time' fits."

"Yeah, yeah, I guess it does." Parker leaned over and tugged Megan's hair. "Maybe I'll start cooking more often, then. I know! Tomorrow, I'll make your favorite and we can have leftovers all week. A huge pot of bean soup with ham hocks. Your grandmother's recipe."

"That is not my favorite! And Erin doesn't like it, either." Wrinkling her nose, she looked at Nicole. "Do you know what ham hocks are, Miss Bradshaw? Pig feet! Yuck."

"Hmm. You loved that soup until your grandmother told you that bit of information, so I think your dislike isn't based on actual taste, kiddo. Just the thought of eating pig's feet."

"Sorry, Dad, but I'm on your daughter's side," Nicole said, laughing again. "Just put normal parts of the pig in your soup, and I'm sure there won't be any problems. Right, Megan?"

"Right!"

This was nice, how easily Nicole seemed to fall in with the family bantering. It was a small thing, but important. "I'll take that under advisement," he said, "but make zero promises."

Margaret Foster came to their table with a handful of menus, which she quickly passed out. "Well, hello there, Lennox family and..." She paused, looked at Nicole with curiosity. "Why, you're Ryan's sister, aren't you? So nice to see you again."

"I am Ryan's sister," Nicole said. "We met at Ryan and Andi's wedding. It's been a while, though, and I guess I didn't connect the dots. How are you?"

"Wait a minute," Parker said, completely lost. "Who is Andi?"

"Andrea is my niece," Margaret supplied. "You were visiting your parents in Florida when Andi and Ryan got married, I think, Parker. Nice that you two have met now, though."

He shouldn't be surprised. Everyone in Steamboat Springs seemed to be connected, in one way or another. "Well, it's a small world, isn't it?"

"She's our new music teacher! And we're helping her find Roscoe, 'cause he ran away last night. Oh. Roscoe is her dog. See?" Erin showed Margaret the sign. "We made these and we saved the last one for you. Daddy said you'd put it up so people can see what Roscoe looks like."

"Yes, I see," Margaret said, taking a closer look at the poster. "You girls did a wonderful job, and of course we'll put this up. I'm thinking right by the door so everyone who comes in and out is sure to notice it." She turned her attention toward Nicole. "I'm so sorry your dog is missing, Nicole. I hope you find him soon."

"Thank you," Nicole said. "I hope the same."

Margaret rattled off the day's specials, which included French onion soup, chicken potpie, and hot roast beef sandwiches with gravy and mashed potatoes. After taking their beverage order, she said, "Do you need a few minutes to look over the menu?"

"Um… I'm set, and I know Erin is." Parker gave a questioning look toward Megan and Nicole. "What about you two? Need some more time or—"

As it turned out, they didn't. Nicole ordered the soup and a side salad, Megan ended up going with her typical—a BLT on toast and chips—Parker went with the roast beef sandwich and Erin stuck with her first choice of chicken strips and fries. After the orders were given and Margaret had walked away, he said to Nicole, "When we're done here, I was thinking we could return to the car and drive the path we already took before going a bit farther out. We can go back to walking then, but I think we've exhausted the immediate area near the school."

"That's a good idea, and I am so grateful for all the help, but I'm guessing the girls might be getting bored looking for a dog they've never even met," Nicole said. "Maybe just drop me off at home after this, and I can wrangle my parents to help. And then you guys—" she smiled at Erin and Megan "—can enjoy the rest of your day doing something a lot more fun."

"But being with you is fun," Megan said. "And we like helping."

"We'll be happier to keep looking, Miss Bradshaw," Erin said. "We almost hit you with our car, so maybe you would've caught Roscoe if that hadn't happened. We should help!"

Before Nicole could toss out any new objections, Parker said, "You should listen to them, as in a way, this is our fault. Well, mine, seeing how neither of the girls were behind the wheel." Instinctively, he leaned over the table and grasped one of Nicole's hands. And there it was, that jolt of lightning the second his skin touched hers. Crazy. Wonderful. Curious. "Unless you're tired of our company, we're in this to the end. You have the Lennox team on your side."

"Team Lennox, huh?" she asked, her tone soft and her eyes warm. Pale pink flooded her cheeks, but she kept her hand tucked into his. He liked that. Perhaps he liked it a little too much, a little too quickly. "I'm honored. So, okay, then, I rescind my offer of escape."

Neither moved for a second. Their gazes stayed connected. And if he'd known her for longer than he had, if his daughters weren't sitting at the same table in rapt attention, he might continue to follow his instincts and kiss her for the next five or fifteen or five hundred minutes. Such a kiss would lead to a flurry of admissions that shouldn't be said. Not yet, anyway, and maybe not ever. That, he knew, would depend on many unpredictable factors.

But he wanted to tell her how she'd impacted him, how she made him feel in a way he hadn't believed he'd ever experience again and how he would very much like to continue forward to explore what those responses might mean. If anything. But she was his kids' music teacher. She was new in town. He knew almost nothing about her past. Hell, she might have a boyfriend. Or a dozen men waiting in the wings. Okay, unlikely. He sincerely doubted she was the type of woman who would be comfortable dating more than one man at a time.

Yet, the facts were undeniable. He didn't know nearly enough.

Releasing her hand, he settled back in his chair. The desire to kiss Nicole, to taste her lips and weave his fingers into her silky mane of blond hair didn't fade. Neither did the desire to, well, confess his attraction, he supposed, so they were on the same page. He felt the need to rush, to claim her *now*, before even another second elapsed.

Ridiculous, of course, for many reasons. Too fast. Too much. Too soon. He could be misinterpreting his body's signals for one thing. For another, Nicole would bolt if he breathed so much as a syllable of what he was thinking, feeling, after only knowing each other for a handful of hours. Rushing would be stupid and foolhardy and could create a gigantic mess.

Just because he hadn't had enough time with Bridget did *not* mean he wouldn't with this woman. Slow and simple; fun and easy. One conversation, one date, one *step* at a time. Like normal people behaved when they were interested in someone. People whose lives hadn't been blown to smithereens by the cancer bomb or a skiing accident or some other arbitrary act of fate.

Fine. It had taken a while, but Parker had found normalcy with his kids, his friends, his job—every other piece of his friggin' life. He could find it here, too.

"Good," he said, picking up the trail of their conversation. *Be normal.* "Because Team Lennox doesn't believe in escape. We choose our positions and we stick."

"Yep! Like glue," Megan said. "Super sticky glue. The kind that doesn't wash off."

Another laugh from Nicole. "Fingernail polish remover does the trick, but seeing how I don't happen to have a bottle on me, I'll agree to be a temporary member of the Lennox team."

"We don't take on temporary members. You're permanently in the fold now," he said, only partially teasing. "As a friend and the girls' music teacher. There are rules, however, and meetings every other Saturday at four o'clock sharp." He winked at his daughters, hoping they'd play along. "Tell her what happens if she's late to the meetings, girls."

Erin scrunched her nose in consideration. "You have to bring pizza if you're late."

"And…you also have to," Megan said, catching on to the joke, "sing to us!"

"Hmm. Pizza and singing if I'm late?" Yet another laugh, this one sweet and almost carefree, slipped from her mouth. "That's quite the punishment! What happens if I'm on time?"

"I guess you'll have to show up to one to find out," Parker said just as Margaret brought their food to the table. "Pizza and singing might not sound like a punishment, but you should know the truth. We make you sing for hours on end while we eat the pizza and watch."

"You know," she said a few minutes later, over a bite of her soup, "there are a few work-arounds that come to mind, so I'm not all that worried."

One brow rose. "Is that so? Details, please."

"Simple. I'll eat before I get there, and you didn't specify what type of pizza I had to bring, which means the toppings are completely my choice." She gave him a teasing smirk. "I'm thinking an anchovy...no, make that sardine, pineapple and...hmm, broccoli pizza with barbecue sauce. Maybe with feta cheese instead of mozzarella."

"Gross!" Megan grimaced. "I won't eat that. I like pepperoni."

To which, Erin said, "Pepperoni and mushroom pizza is the best."

"Oh, don't you worry," Nicole said with a conspiratorial wink, "I'll bring you girls whatever you want. The sardine specialty is meant for your father's enjoyment."

Robust laughter burst from Parker's chest. This woman was something. Beautiful, sweet, smart and sexy. Compassionate and real. There didn't seem to be a fake bone in her body. Depth, he guessed he'd call it. All of that combined was more than enough, by a long shot. Add in her sense of humor? Her ability to connect with his daughters? Perfection. "I'll eat whatever you put in front of me, Nicole, even that revolting mess you just described."

A moment of silence ensued before she shrugged. "Well, that isn't fun at all, and I don't believe you for a second. Someday, I might have to test you on that claim."

Someday sounded good. The barbecue pineapple, sardine and broccoli pizza? Not so much. But what he said was "Sure. I'll choke it down while you sing."

"Have you considered that I might be a horrible

singer? Just because I'm a music teacher doesn't mean I can carry a tune. Imagine listening to a howling, feral cat for an hour." Another shrug, but her eyes—oh, they were all but glowing, and that smile of hers was as bright as the sun. Good. She needed the reprieve. "This little punishment idea of yours could easily backfire."

"Don't believe her, Daddy!" Erin almost jumped out of her seat in her enthusiasm to tattle on her teacher. "She sings in class with the rest of us, and she sounds wonderful."

He bet she did. Like an angel, was his guess. A firecracker of an angel who had piqued more than his interest. In less than twenty-four hours, even. It had to mean something. His job was figuring out what. Well, that, and bringing Roscoe safely home. Tonight preferably, because he hated the thought of Nicole being sad and scared and lonely.

Yeah. He really hated that thought.

Monday morning, Nicole sat on her kitchen floor and stared at Roscoe's food and water bowls. She'd automatically filled them, had even called for him, before remembering the awful truth. He wasn't here. They hadn't found him on Saturday or on Sunday, when Team Lennox had insisted on joining her search efforts yet again. She hadn't argued.

They wanted to help. She wanted their help. It was less lonely and scary with Parker, and the girls' positive attitudes and silly banter made the process feel lighter and happier. Despite all of that, and the combined hopeful determination of four, a miracle had not occurred.

How could a dog that large and loud and loving—and, well, she thought he was beautiful, but others described him as rather homely—disappear without anyone seeing him? It didn't make sense.

This morning, she had felt Roscoe's loss, knew he wasn't here, but she'd fallen into her normal before-school routine and had filled his food and water bowls, had called his name and had waited several excruciating seconds before realizing what she had done, that he was not here, and that she had no idea where else to look or what else to do.

And while different on many levels, this reminded her of being ill. Of doing every last thing the doctor told her to do and knowing she couldn't do anything else but hope and pray. Whatever happened next was out of her hands. It felt awful then and it felt awful now.

She sat on the floor, arms wrapped around her bent legs, and sobbed while staring at Roscoe's food and water bowls, wishing she could reverse time and keep him from running off in the first place. An impossible wish, so she focused on the hours immediately ahead of her. She had a job to get to. Kids to teach. Tryouts to reschedule. Moping about what couldn't be changed wouldn't help. Staying busy, however, might. She wiped the tears from her cheeks, called the shelters—no luck there—and finished getting ready for work.

The morning passed swiftly enough, but her heart remained heavy. Especially as she explained to the students in each of her classes why the Christmas play tryouts had been postponed at the last minute. Kids tended to ask a lot of questions, and by and large, they liked dogs. Which meant that she was continually talking about Roscoe, keeping him front and center in her thoughts. Every chance she had, she'd check her phone for any missed calls. None.

She hid in her classroom during her lunch break, eating at her desk and looking at a map of Steamboat Springs, trying to think like a dog. Nothing new or helpful came to mind.

He liked people, running, playing, squeaky toys and, naturally, food. He liked to burrow under the blankets and sleep at her feet, sit at the front window and stare at birds and rabbits and passing pedestrians and cars. He liked to rest his head on her lap when she watched TV, nuzzle into her when she was sad or scared and steal her shoes if she didn't put them away. All of that explained his personality but gave her no clues to where he was.

The bell rang, signaling the change in periods, and Nicole had managed to eat only a third of her sandwich. That was fine; she didn't have much of an appetite. She cleaned up and checked her phone again—still nothing—and prepared herself for an afternoon of more explaining, more questions, more thinking about her dog.

Kids started piling into the classroom, some chattering and some quiet as they took their seats, and seconds before the bell rang, the final group arrived. Erin was among them, and she came directly to Nicole, her expression unsure. Oh. Nicole should've realized that after spending the weekend together like they had, returning to the student-teacher relationship might seem odd for the girls. While Megan had seemed fine earlier—she was in one of the morning classes—Erin was older, and therefore, was somewhat more aware of relationship boundaries.

"Hi, Erin." She smiled in hopes of putting the ten-year-old at ease. "It feels a little strange today, being back in the classroom after the weekend, doesn't it?"

"A little, yeah." Darting her brown-eyed gaze downward, she tugged at her shirt that was emblazoned with the words *GIRLS RULE* and said, "What about Roscoe? Did you find him last night or this morning? I hope you did."

"Not yet, Erin, no," Nicole said, keeping her voice low. "Listen, there's nothing to feel weird about, okay? I'm your teacher during school hours, but I'm also your friend."

The girl's shoulders relaxed and she looked up with a smile. "That's what Daddy said, but I didn't know. We...me and Megan, I mean...wanted to help you again after school, but we have to go to my aunt's house for dinner. Daddy says we have homework and other obligations."

"Well, I appreciate the offer, but your father is right," Nicole said in a gentle tone. "You have already helped a ton, homework is a priority and I bet your aunt and cousins miss you."

"I know all that. But I bet if you called Daddy and told him you really wanted our help, he'd say yes. And we could go see Aunt Daisy and the twins tomorrow."

Swallowing a sigh, Nicole patted Erin's arm. "I'm sure you're right, but I don't think that's very fair, do you? It's your dad's job to do what is best for you and your sister. And honestly," she said, "I don't know where else to look. Over the last two days, we've pretty much covered the entirety of Steamboat Springs. I… think he might be in someone's house or garage."

"That's what Daddy said, too." Sighing, Erin said, "Okay. We'll do our homework and visit with Aunt Daisy, Uncle Reid and the twins. But If Roscoe isn't back by this weekend, can we help more then? Please? Daddy said that was up to you."

How to answer that one? Yes, if she continued searching by foot, she'd welcome the girls' company— not to mention their father's—but if Roscoe hadn't returned after a full week, walking around as they already had didn't hold much logic. Other than, perhaps, putting up more signs with his picture and her contact information.

"Right now, we need to start class," she said, "but I'm not sure what the next step is. Let's hold off on making that decision until we see what the week brings. Sound okay?"

Nodding, Erin retreated to her chair, and Nicole faced the class, again going through her apologies and explanation of what had happened at the play tryouts on Friday. After questions were answered, she moved through the day's lesson, which involved a game that would help the kids learn how to identify musical pitches. It went well, as did the rest of her afternoon classes.

When the final bell rang and the day was done, Nicole—as she had all day—checked her phone. No missed calls, but she had a text from Parker that read, Any news?

She replied, None at all. Thanks for checking, though!

In less than a minute, he responded with:

Easy to check in. You're on my mind. So is Roscoe. Was hoping for good news. I'm sorry, Nicole.

It's okay! It wasn't, not yet, but either Roscoe would show up soon, and her statement would become true, or he wouldn't return and she'd eventually be okay. Either way, it was considerate that Parker had thought to check in. She stared at her phone for another few seconds, bit her lip and texted, Heading home now. Enjoy the rest of your day.

And of course, she took the long way home, keeping her eye out for Roscoe. Just in case he had been stuck in someone's garage and was now wandering the streets. When a miracle did not occur, tears built and her throat clogged, but she pushed through the emotion. She couldn't do anything she hadn't already done. Time to go home.

Chapter Five

Parker picked up Erin and Megan from school and took them to his sister's house. Daisy and Reid were going to spend the rest of the afternoon with them, feed them dinner and make sure they finished their home-work. He had a WebEx meeting with a client at five, and it was expected to last a couple of hours. While he occasionally brought work home, his clients deserved his full attention for meetings and consults, so he held those at his office.

Normally, he tried to plan around the girls' school hours, but schedules didn't always align, and when that happened, Daisy stepped in to help. It was strange now to think of the years she'd lived in California. Eight of them, to be exact, and other than holidays and the oc-casional phone calls, those were years they weren't a part of each other's lives. She'd fled on her wedding day—her original wedding day, that was—and had left his best friend and her jilted groom, Reid, devastated. Back then, he'd stood by Reid and hadn't tried to mend fences with Daisy, hadn't really tried to discover what had sent her running. He hadn't been there for her.

All those wasted years. He should have found a way to be there for both Daisy and Reid. It had taken Bridget's death, followed by the skiing accident that had nearly killed him, to reach out to Daisy, to bring her home. Water under the bridge now, he supposed. She and Reid were together and happy, and his relationship with Daisy had become stronger than ever.

Back at his office with a little over an hour to spare before the official start of the meeting, Parker grabbed a bottle of water and buckled down to work. He kept at it until the timer for the meeting had hit the ten-minute mark, and began the log-in process. He had barely typed in his name when he received an apologetic text from his client. An unexpected opportunity had dropped into his lap, so he would have to reschedule the meeting for another time. Parker's first response was slight annoyance, but on the heels of that another thought materialized.

And oh, it was a tempting thought.

His girls were settled for the next few hours. Why not stop by and personally check in on Nicole? That would be far better than a text. He could give her a call first, see if she'd eaten dinner yet, and if not, maybe they could go out or he could just bring over a couple of burgers. They'd be able to talk one-on-one, maybe dig beneath the surface a little and learn some of those facts he was missing. Lord, the idea tempted. Again, more than it should.

Parker swallowed half of his water in one long gulp, considered giving in to the temptation, but common sense prevailed. They had just spent two full days in each other's company. She was probably tired, worried about Roscoe, and while he'd like to think he could make her smile, maybe even laugh, to lighten that burden for a few minutes, showing up with barely any notice, twice in as few days, didn't seem the best plan.

For either of them, really.

Decision made, Parker locked the office and headed to his car. He'd join his family for dinner, spend some valuable time with his sister and brother-in-law, his niece and nephew, and then take the girls home for their evening routine. In the car, he buckled his seat belt, trying to get thoughts of a disheveled angel out of his head. Trying not to think of her feeling lonely, missing the company of her dog, and... Yeah, that wasn't going to work.

She was in his head. He might as well accept the reality of that.

Leaving the parking lot, he started to turn right, which would lead him in the direction of his sister's house, when he swerved left, instead. It was growing dark, but he had a good thirty minutes of light left. Might as well drive by the school, the streets that surrounded the building, before going to Daisy's. He'd done the same this morning, and again before he'd picked up the girls that afternoon. There wasn't a lot he could do for Nicole, but he could do this.

Half an hour later, Parker sighed in disappointment. If they weren't at Daisy's too late, he'd do another swing with the girls on their way home. They'd like that, being involved. And they loved dogs, wanted one of their own, but Parker kept putting them off. It wasn't that he disliked dogs. He liked them well enough. But adding one more responsibility to their household didn't rank high on his want-to-do list, and he kept telling himself that they spent enough time with Jinx to fill that need. Selfish on his part? Perhaps a little.

Christmas wasn't that far off. Maybe he should give the idea of a puppy some serious consideration. The girls were responsible enough to help, and he could almost hear their squeals of joy now. He smiled at the image of them on Christmas morning, coming downstairs to find a puppy—or maybe he'd go the route his sister had and adopt a dog from a rescue shelter—with a big red bow around his neck, sitting under the tree. Yeah, that would make their Christmas.

He was driving through the center of Steamboat Springs when he saw a large, lumbering animal on the side of the road. A deer, he thought. Slowing down, he veered to the opposite side of the lane, watching carefully in case the deer startled and jumped in front of the car. But the headlights didn't spook him at all. In fact, he sat down on his haunches and tipped his head toward the light, just as Parker drove past. And even then, it took an extra few seconds for the image to register in Parker's brain. That wasn't a deer.

It was a dog. A large dog, at that. Maybe even part moose.

Could he be that lucky? Pulling off to the side of the road, Parker all but leaped from the car and jogged toward the dog, who still sat on his haunches, tail wagging, watching his approach with calm alertness. And as he got closer, he was about as certain as he could be that, yeah, somehow, he'd gotten that lucky. He'd stared at this dog's picture for the past two days, hadn't he? Was it possible there were two missing moose-dogs in the vicinity?

Possible, if highly doubtful. The tags would be the absolute proof.

"Roscoe? Is that you, boy?" And yup, that tail wagged even harder. Reaching the dog, who hadn't budged an inch, despite Nicole's assertion that Roscoe loved to run, Parker knelt and held out his hand. A quick sniff and a lick later, he felt for the tags on the dog's collar.

They were there, but he couldn't read them in the darkness. Didn't matter. Parker wouldn't leave him out here, regardless of his identity. He belonged to someone, even if that someone wasn't Nicole. Standing, Parker gently took hold of the dog's collar.

"Come on, boy," he said with a slight tug. "Come with me, and we'll see what we can do about getting you home. And if you are Roscoe, I can guarantee a meal fit for a king. Nicole will probably broil you a steak and cover it with bacon. And smother you with hugs and kisses."

A whine emerged from the dog's throat, as if in agreement, and surprisingly, he followed Parker to the car without any trouble or so much as a sign that he was prepping for escape. Either Roscoe had exhausted himself over the past few days or this wasn't Roscoe.

Parker hoped like hell for the former.

When he opened the passenger door to the front seat, the dog climbed in, sitting straight and tall. Whined again, a long and imploring sound, as if to say, "What are you waiting for? Check my tags and get me home. Now, already!"

"I'm getting there." Parker scratched the dog's head, eliciting another whine. "Needed to make sure you weren't going to take off again." And then, with a quick prayer, he leaned over and read the tag. Unexpected emotion—sappy, at that—hit him with the strength of a semi blasting down the highway. He cleared his throat, blinked and gave Roscoe another scratch on his head. "Nice to meet you, Roscoe. Finally. Let's get you back to Nicole, shall we?"

That damn lump of emotion stayed lodged in Parker's throat as he drove toward Nicole's. There was happiness there, obviously, for Nicole. Gratitude, as well. But also a sense that he'd somehow stepped straight into the Twilight Zone because, of all the people in Steamboat Springs who could've found Roscoe, it had been Parker. The chances of that had to be one in a million, if not one in two million. Toss in the rest: how he met Nicole, how she made him feel, how he yearned to see to her well-being, and he had to be hovering somewhere in the impossible range of statistics. But he *had* found Roscoe, through one of those twists of fate.

A good one, this time. Hell, more than good. He'd hit the jackpot.

The house creaked with the weight of silence. To compensate for all the quiet, Nicole had Billy Joel playing while she finished preparing dinner. Comfort food in the form of spaghetti and meatballs and garlic bread with melted provolone. She'd decided to live dangerously and skip a side salad. She could get her greens in tomorrow, or the day after.

Tonight, though, was about relaxing with a bowlful of carbs and her favorite musical, *My Fair Lady*. If she had a sofa, she'd wrap herself in a blanket and curl up with some pillows. But she hadn't bought one yet, so she'd settle for a chair. Or the floor, with a pile of pillows and blankets, if she wanted to stretch out. Between the movie and the carbs, she hoped to lull herself into a sleep coma that would last until her alarm blared.

Maybe tomorrow, she'd get her miracle.

With the sauce and meatballs simmering and the spaghetti close to being done, she slid the garlic bread into the preheated oven and then retrieved the colander from the cupboard. And like that morning, her muscle memory kept kicking in. She'd step over the places Roscoe usually camped himself while she was cooking, or she'd break off a piece of cheese and drop her hand, expecting him to be right there, waiting for any little tidbit she'd pass his way.

If he wasn't found, how long would it take her body to catch on?

Shoving the unpleasant, if becoming more possible by the minute, speculation into the ether, Nicole dumped the spaghetti into the colander. The cheese on the garlic bread was melted and bubbly, so she turned off the oven and pulled out the baking sheet. Dinner was ready. A small victory, but she'd take it. She filled a plate with a great deal more than she'd likely eat, exchanged Billy Joel for her Blu-ray disc of *My Fair Lady* and settled herself in a chair.

Five minutes into her meal and the movie, her doorbell rang. It wasn't late—only a little after six—but she didn't have many visitors other than her family. And she tended to know when they were stopping by. Parker and the girls? Maybe. Probably.

A shiver of anticipation, excitement, rolled through her body. Her skin warmed and her lips stretched into a smile. She carried her plate to the front door, reminding herself that Parker's presence—if he was her visitor—was probably a result of endless pleading from his daughters.

The doorbell rang a second time as she unlocked and swung open the door. And there he stood, in blue jeans and a black jacket, with wind-tousled hair and a wide, almost-exuberant smile. That smile, the tousled hair—the very look of him caught her attention so fully that, initially, he was all she saw. A portion of her loneliness, sadness, dissolved and disappeared. It seemed she hadn't needed comfort food or *My Fair Lady* to feel better.

Parker Lennox appearing on her front porch did the job.

She opened her mouth to greet him when finally—*finally*—her brain clicked into gear and she noticed he was slightly hunched over, his hand holding on to a dog. Oh. *Oh.* Her dog. Her Roscoe. She let go of her plate, sending sauce, meatballs and pasta flying all over the front porch, but she didn't care. Her dog was here.

With a yelp of happiness, she dropped to her knees and wrapped her arms around Roscoe's furry neck, pulling him in for a tight hug. He whined in her ear and then slathered her cheek with wet kisses. "Where have you been?" she said, half crying, half laughing as she ran her hands down his back. His fur was matted, but she didn't feel any actual injuries. Later, she'd check him more thoroughly. "And don't you ever disappear again."

Disengaging from her grasp, Roscoe licked her cheek again before inhaling the scattered remains of her dinner from his immediate vicinity. She stood and looked at Parker, who still hadn't uttered so much as a syllable. The girls weren't with him, she realized, which meant they were still at their aunt's. "Hi," she said as their gazes connected. "You found him, Parker."

He smiled. "Hi there, Nicole. I'm not all that sure I found him, but yeah, here he is."

Relief and joy and gratitude collided into a huge pile of emotion that couldn't be—shouldn't be—ignored. She threw herself at him, wrapped her arms around him and held on just as tightly as she had with Roscoe. "You found him, Parker," she repeated in a sob, her face pressed against his coat and her words colliding into one another. "You found him and you brought him home. Thank you, thank you, thank you."

"Aw, Nicole, you're welcome," he said, his voice low. "Truth is, I didn't so much find him as he found me, almost as if he knew where to be at the precisely right moment."

"Really?" She retreated a few inches, wiped her tears. "That's a story I need to hear. Let me get him inside so I can look him over and... I'm just so happy you found him."

"Me, too. And, Nicole?" he said, still holding on to Roscoe's collar with his right hand. "You have a little something—" he rubbed his other thumb over her chin "—right here."

"Spaghetti sauce, I'm guessing." His touch, as light and quick as it was, brought forth another round of shivers. "Um. I only had a few bites before decorating my porch, and I have enough for a few more servings. Have you eaten? I'll feed you dinner and you can tell me how you found Roscoe. Unless... Is your sister expecting you?"

"I have an hour or two, and dinner sounds good."

Anticipation caused a delicious flurry of warmth in her belly. To hide her reaction and to stop herself from doing something really crazy—like planting a kiss on his lips—she retrieved her plate and fork from the porch and then motioned for Parker to follow her inside.

My Fair Lady was still playing. She turned it off with a flick of the remote and, once everyone was in the kitchen, put her dirty plate in the sink. Roscoe rushed his food and water bowls, attacking them with a vengeance, while Parker took off his coat and leaned against the wall, saying, "First things first. Check over your dog. Make sure he's okay."

Nodding, Nicole sat on the floor and waited for the dog to finish eating. While she waited, she tried to think of something to say to Parker, other than more thank-yous, but failed. When her dog seemed to have his fill, she said, "Come here, Roscoe, let's see the damage."

He huffed loudly, as if in exasperation, but padded to her in slow, even movements. She started with his head, carefully moving her hands over his body and then to his legs and paws, searching for any bumps or cuts. Other than his obvious exhaustion and losing a few pounds, he seemed in pretty good shape. Better than she would've expected.

She gave him another tight hug. "I think you're okay, but to be absolutely sure, we'll go see the veterinarian this week. And a bath later tonight, buddy, along with some brushing time."

Another huff, this one louder than the last, before he gave in to his exhaustion and crumpled on the floor, closing his eyes. Based on the dog snores, he fell asleep instantly.

"Tired dog," Parker said. "Wonder how much walking he's done over the past few days, who he has met and what he has seen. Quite the explorer, your Roscoe."

Releasing a sigh, Nicole stood and washed her hands. "Yeah, and his wanderlust nature has just earned him house arrest for the next good long while. He'll have to make do with exploring the backyard until I forget about this experience." If she ever did. Her earlier fear returned, washing through her with acute ferocity. "He scared me. I was beginning to think..."

That she'd lost him. Forever.

"I know. But he's here, safe and sound."

Retrieving two clean plates from the cupboard, she let the truth of that sink in. "Yes, and that's all that matters. Tell me how you found him? I'll get our dinner as you do."

So, while Parker explained the events that led to Roscoe's rescue, she filled their plates with pasta and sauce, microwaved them one at a time and, every now and then, asked him a question. It was rather extraordinary, how he'd happened to be in just the right place at the right time. That Roscoe hadn't run off again as Parker approached, and that the dog had so easily followed him to his car. To Nicole, in her frame of mind, a miracle had occurred.

"I'm so glad you knew what he looks like," she said, bringing their plates to the table. "What do you want to drink? I have water, milk and raspberry iced tea. Pick your poison."

"Milk is good, and thank you, Nicole." Parker sat down at the table. "This looks delicious. I saw, when I came in, that you were watching *My Fair Lady*. We can do that, if you want, while we eat. Or we can talk. You get to choose, since you cooked."

She wanted to talk to this man for hours, but she was also exhausted, drained and afraid of what she might say in her current state. So, she went with the safe, if cowardly choice. "If you don't mind, I'd like to just veg in front of the TV. We can watch something else, though."

"I can't stay for the entire movie, but I'm fine with *My Fair Lady*." He stood, with his plate and milk in hand, and walked toward the living room. Over his shoulder, he said, "Haven't seen that one in a while, but it was one of Bridget's favorites. And the girls love *The Sound of Music*. Bet they'd enjoy this one, too."

"Oh. They probably would."

When they entered the living room, he chuckled before choosing one of the chairs. "You need a couch, Nicole. Something large and comfortable, so you can curl up."

"I know," she said. "I keep meaning to buy one, but something else always seems to interrupt that plan." Like her dog running away.

For the next hour or so, they ate their dinner and sat in companionable silence, watching Audrey Hepburn and Rex Harrison do their thing. It wasn't awkward or uncomfortable in any way, and by the time Parker had to leave, she wished she'd chosen conversation over the movie. Wished she'd taken the opportunity to get to know him better, rather than the easy way out.

Well, maybe there would be a next time.

At the front door, she thanked him again for bringing Roscoe home, asked him to give the girls the good news, and for about five seconds, she had the wild wish that he'd kiss her. Of course, he didn't. Just smiled and nodded and told her to have a good night.

And then he was gone. She watched as he pulled out of her driveway, her thoughts jumping every which way. She liked Parker Lennox. A lot. And maybe, just maybe, she shouldn't rule out the possibility of another miracle. Two more, to be exact.

Hope for the best. Why not?

Chapter Six

Sitting with the other parents in the school auditorium, Parker waited for the girls to take their turn at the rescheduled Christmas play tryouts. Like last Friday, he'd picked them up from school and taken them to Fosters Bar and Grill for dinner before returning here. Unlike last Friday, he did not have a near collision with an angel and her dog.

It was crazy, to think of all that had occurred within the past seven days.

Since Monday evening, when he'd left Nicole's, they'd texted here and there throughout the rest of the week. Nothing serious, all light, but he looked forward to and enjoyed the contact. Tonight, also unlike last week, she had chosen to leave Roscoe at home, which did not surprise him. Other than the visit to the vet,

Nicole had kept the dog under house arrest, just as she said she would. She seemed, to Parker, a woman who meant what she said and said what she meant.

He liked that, too, as he'd never been a fan of mixed messages.

They had arrived at the school early enough for Parker to get a front-row seat, which meant he could easily see and hear everything that took place onstage. Watching Nicole, who had chosen to forgo the angel getup for a pair of jeans and a pink turtleneck, and knowing her as he now did, he recognized her nerves when she first approached the microphone to address the kids and their parents. Her voice shook, just a little, when she explained the change in play choice for this year. Everyone seemed on board and excited about presenting *A Christmas Carol* using fairy-tale characters, and the longer she spoke, the more comfortable she became. By the time the actual tryouts started, she'd found her groove.

So, he kicked back and enjoyed watching the kids as one after another stepped into the various roles up for grabs. Well, two roles per character, really, since the kids would have to pull off playing Rumpelstiltskin as Ebenezer Scrooge, Pinocchio as Bob Cratchit, Snow White as the Ghost of Christmas Past, and a variety of other dual personalities.

He leaned forward when he heard Erin's name called. With the change in play, he didn't know which role either of his girls would want, but he guessed one of the princesses. At least now, he didn't have to worry about only one of his daughters becoming an angel.

Now he had to hope that they both weren't aiming for Snow White or Red Riding Hood.

Nicole had Erin read the same handful of dialogue the other kids before her had read, and she handled it like a pro. She articulated well and spoke in a loud, clear voice, even adding some personality to her tone when called for. And he thought of Bridget, as he did often where the girls were concerned, and how she would be grinning ear to ear and beaming with pride. She'd nudge his side and say something like, "That's our daughter up there! Look at her!"

Loss kicked him squarely in the gut, at the unfairness of it all. Bridget deserved to be here, and their girls absolutely deserved to have their mother.

Three kids followed Erin before it was Megan's turn, and again, Parker leaned forward in anticipation and pride. Megan was obviously more nervous than Erin had been, but she was also several years younger. At first, she spoke so low that her voice was barely audible from Parker's position. By the third line of dialogue, though, he could hear her just fine. And when she was done, she smiled big and bright before dipping into a perfect curtsy and sashaying off stage.

"Ah, Bridget," Parker whispered. "They were incredible. You would have loved this."

Five minutes later, the girls silently took the seats on either side of him, and together they watched the rest of the tryouts. On the way over, they had decided to stay until the end, even though they could have left now that the girls were done. Parker was pleased, because staying meant he could talk with Nicole, and his daughters, well, they were just excited to be here.

Within another thirty minutes, tryouts were over and everyone was leaving, ready to start their weekend. Parker, with Erin and Megan following, joined Nicole on the stage. She looked up as she tucked the script pages and her notebook into a blue-and-white-striped tote bag.

"Need help with anything?" Parker asked, noticing right off that she looked tired. Happy, though, too. So, the good type of tired. "We have six hands, ready to do your bidding."

"All I need is for these four chairs to be folded and returned backstage," Nicole said with a smile directed at Erin and Megan. "Think you girls can handle that? I'll even offer a reward. Ice cream and a visit with Roscoe at my house when you're done, if your dad agrees."

"Yes!" Megan said, already folding a chair. "Please, Daddy? Ice cream and Roscoe!"

"He'll say yes." Erin folded a chair. "He likes Miss Bradshaw."

"Daddy? Yes, please?"

Parker laughed. "Yes."

Megan squealed and Erin gave her sister an I-told-you-so look as they walked toward the back of the stage, each lugging a chair behind them.

"So, you like me, huh?" Nicole asked. "Or is it really all about the ice cream?"

"Depends," he deadpanned. "What flavor of ice cream are we talking about? Makes a difference, you know. Vanilla, then you're definitely the reason I said yes."

She grinned and dipped her head, hiding her eyes. Too bad. He loved seeing her eyes when she smiled. They seemed to sparkle. "Good to know I'm more interesting than vanilla."

"Oh, without a doubt. Now, chocolate on the other hand... I'd have to give it some consideration. Might be a tie." He waited a beat, hoping she'd glance at him. When she didn't, he continued with "And strawberry is my favorite. Tell me you have strawberry ice cream, and we have a real dilemma on our hands. Ranking wise, that is."

"Sorry," she said, just as the girls returned to grab the last two chairs, "no strawberry. But I am curious what your thoughts are on chocolate peppermint swirl or cookies and cream." Now she tipped her chin, and their gazes met, and there was that fire. He wanted to get her alone, explore what that fire meant. Where it might take them. "Ranking wise, that is."

He was this close to teasing her more but decided not to. This mattered, what he said here, even in such a light moment. "Right at the top, Nicole, whatever the flavor of ice cream. Erin was right. I do like you. Quite a bit, actually, and I was wondering if you'd—"

"The chairs are put away!" Megan said, running onto the stage with her sister. "So we're ready to meet Roscoe and have ice cream. Do you think he'll play with us, Miss Bradshaw?"

"Um. Yes, of course he will," Nicole said, her gaze remaining locked with Parker's. Curiosity and something else—interest perhaps?—slipped into her expression. A rosy pink blush appeared on her cheeks, and the air between them seemed to crackle with electricity. She bit her lip, a little action that instantly drove Parker ten ways of crazy. She blinked and focused on Megan. "Roscoe will probably wear you girls out, he likes to play so much."

Happy and excited, Megan ran down the stage steps to get her coat from her seat. Erin, after a moment's hesitation, did the same. "Well, I guess they're ready," Parker said to Nicole. He held his hand toward her. "Shall we? And thank you, by the way, for the invitation."

"We should. And you're welcome." She didn't put her hand in his, but instead, she gave him the tote bag, which broadened his smile. "It is the very least I can do."

"Nah. You don't owe us anything." They joined the girls, and together all four walked out of the building into the parking lot. "Team Lennox, remember? Helping is part of the deal."

"Well, then, so is ice cream," she said when they reached her car. Retrieving her tote bag, she tossed it in the back seat. Then, "I'll see you guys in a few minutes!"

"Okay, Miss Bradshaw!" Megan tugged on Parker's hand. "Let's go, Daddy!"

They returned to their car, and once everyone was buckled in, Parker turned on the engine and followed Nicole out of the parking lot. "So, you both did an incredible job at the tryouts," he said. "I'm very proud of you, and I know your mom would be, too."

"She is," Megan said with absolute authority. "She watches us from heaven, you know."

"Does she, Daddy?" Erin asked. "For real, I mean. Can she do that?"

Parker released a breath. A pat answer wouldn't do, so he did the best he could with "No one can say for sure, pumpkin, but I can tell you this…if there is any way for your mother to watch over you girls, trust me, she is. She loved you fiercely, with every bone in her body."

"I know she watches us," Megan said. "She wrote that in her letter to us."

Bridget had written a handful of letters to her family before her death, most of which they'd already read, and whenever the girls asked, they'd read again. But there were a few that Bridget had wanted saved for specific occasions: each of the girls' eighteenth birthdays, their first day of college, their wedding days and the births of their first child.

Those letters, Parker had locked away. He would honor her wishes by waiting, and he hadn't even broken the seals on the envelopes. They were from Bridget to her daughters, to be read by them when the time came, and not by him just because he was their father.

"But what if she wrote that because she wanted it to be true, and not because she knew it was true?" Erin asked. "She might have wanted it so much that she believed it."

His eldest daughter, far too wise, too introspective for her age.

"I can't answer that, sweetie," he said, wishing he could give her the definitive response she needed. But he wouldn't lie. "I like to believe she's with us, all of the time."

"Yeah, like Santa Claus," Megan piped up. "If he can see whether we're good or bad, then Mommy can watch us every day, too. She saw us, Erin. I know it!"

"But Santa isn't even real," Erin said. "So—"

"He is too real!" Megan's voice broke. "Tell her, Daddy."

Wow. This conversation had spiraled fast. "I think it's about what you believe," Parker said, choosing his words carefully. Breaking his youngest daughter's heart didn't appeal, and he figured she had a year or two of Santa-filled Christmases left, if he could handle this correctly and one of her friends didn't spill the beans, like one of Erin's had this past Christmas. "When you believe, a sort of magic happens, and in that magic, I think anything can happen."

Both girls were quiet for a few seconds. Then Erin said, her tone wistful, "So if we believe that Mommy can see us and hear us and be around us, maybe she really can?"

"I think that sounds about right, but what do you think?"

"I believe," Megan said. "Erin?"

"I...I...I think that Mommy really liked seeing us try out tonight."

Megan sighed a happy sigh. "That's what I think.

And now she'll get to see us playing with Roscoe and eating ice cream at Miss Bradshaw's! She'll like that, too."

They were less than five minutes from Nicole's, and he wanted their minds on happier topics, so he asked, "Speaking of the tryouts, which parts do you two think you want?"

"Snow White!" they both said at the same time.

"You can't be Snow White," Erin said to Megan. "You're not tall enough, and she—"

"You're not that tall, either, Erin! And yes, I can be Snow White. She had really white skin, and so do I, and she likes birds, and so do I, and..."

Lovely. A full week later and right back to square one.

Two ice-cream-stuffed girls and an overgrown dog were fast asleep on Nicole's bed. She smiled at the sight and covered all three with a blanket. They'd piled in here after their treats, roughhousing and playing with Roscoe, and when suddenly there was an absence of giggles and shrieks streaming into the living room, she came to check on them.

They must have really been worn-out, as it wasn't even eight o'clock yet. Assuming Parker wouldn't wait too much longer to gather them up and head home, she took a few extra minutes to just look at them, to revel in the idea that someday, it might be her child asleep on this bed, after eating ice cream and playing with Roscoe. Placing her palm on her stomach, Nicole prayed that this time, the procedure had worked. This time in a week, she could take an early response pregnancy test, but she might wait another week or two.

Thanksgiving was six days away, for one thing. She wanted to enjoy the holiday with her family, focus on all she had to be thankful for and not be upset over a negative test. Also, though, since she'd started this journey, every negative test had her peeing on a new stick each morning, in blind hope, until she received the official "not yet" from the fertility clinic. This time, she wanted to save herself from that daily dose of devastation. She just wasn't sure if, when the moment came, she'd be able to resist the temptation.

Closing the door about halfway, she rejoined Parker in the living room, saying, "Nothing nefarious was afoot. They're fast asleep, with the dog curled right in between them. They must have had a busy day, to fall asleep so early. When is their normal bedtime?"

"Eight thirty, no later than nine, during the week, so this isn't that early for them," Parker said, stretching his legs in front of him. "Though, between school and the tryouts, coming here and playing with Roscoe, they did have a fuller day than normal. And we had a tough conversation on the drive over. That may have sapped some of their energy."

"Oh? Is everything okay?" Nicole sat down in the vacant chair and promised herself that tomorrow, come hell or high water, she would buy a sofa. While Parker hadn't mentioned her continued lack of one, she felt somewhat embarrassed. He'd yet to answer her question, so she said, "You can tell me it isn't any of my business and my feelings won't be hurt. I promise."

"It isn't that. I'm just not sure where to start." He gave his head a small shake, let out a breath and said, "We haven't talked about their mother yet, so I don't know what you know."

Why, oh, why had she asked about his conversation with the girls? This wasn't only painful territory, it could become dangerous. But she had asked, he had answered and volleyed a question back at her. So, she told him the truth. "Well, the other teachers have filled me in some, and this is a fairly tight-knit community, so…I know you're a widower. I'm so sorry, Parker."

"Thank you. I'm sorry, too." Combing his fingers through his hair, he said, "I'm not surprised that people talk, that's normal. What have you been told?"

"That your wife died from breast cancer, and that after her death, you and the girls moved here from Boston, since Steamboat Springs is your hometown." She said the words matter-of-factly, as if they didn't hold the weight of the world or a universe of pain and sadness for this man and his daughters. "I would never have brought it up, Parker. This… I'm just very sorry."

"It's okay. It's good to talk about. I forget that sometimes. Anyway," he said, "on the drive here, Erin asked if Bridget—that was my wife's name—could really watch over them from heaven. I wanted to give her the absolute answer she needed. But she's a smart kid, and she'd have asked more questions if I tried to bluff."

"Yes, she would've. Erin likes knowing all the details."

"She does, doesn't she? I went with the truth, which

boiled down to, I don't know, but if there's any possible way, then yes, their mother is watching over them."

Such a tough conversation. She felt for Parker, for the girls, and wished she could somehow heal the wounds they'd suffered. Impossible, of course, but that didn't make the wish disappear. "I think you handled it well. How did Erin take your explanation?"

"She took it well, actually. Decided that their mother had watched them in the tryouts and enjoyed herself." He paused. "On that note, what are the chances of having two Snow Whites in the play? Because, as it turns out, both girls want the same part."

"No chance on two Snow Whites, but—" She broke off, closed her eyes and let herself step onto that dangerous ground. "I should tell you something, I think. I don't want to, really, but...well, let me ask you this first. Earlier, at the school, you started to say something before the girls were done with the chairs. Were you... That is, it seemed as if you were about to—"

"Ask you on a date?" Parker said, his gaze on her, steady and sure. "Yes, Nicole, that is exactly what I was about to do. I think we have a lot in common. I like you, would enjoy getting to know you better, and I don't see any reason not to be clear in my intentions."

She swallowed. Hard. Nodded. "I like you, too, and we do seem to have...a lot in common, and I've enjoyed...well, every minute we've spent together so far."

"There's a 'but' in there, I'm guessing." Parker sighed, combed his fingers through his hair a second time. "If you're not interested in more, or even seeing if there could be more, that's okay. I still like you. So do the girls." A lopsided grin appeared, and she could almost—almost—see what he might have looked like as a little boy. "Friends are good. Good friends are better."

Oh. He just gave her a way out, and she considered—for all of three seconds—taking and running with that out. But she did like him, she was interested in discovering if more could exist between them, she just had to be honest. So he knew the road she'd traveled.

Unfair, with his past, if she didn't. Unfair to the girls. Unfair to her, as well.

So, she pulled together the strands of her courage, inhaled a breath deep into her lungs and said, "I am interested, Parker. But you might not be after I tell you..." Her words trailed off and she swallowed again. "This is harder than I thought," she admitted, "which is ridiculous, really. I don't share this with many people, you see, and...and—"

"Then don't tell me yet, Nicole," Parker said in an easy and calm manner. Steady and sure, like his gaze. "There is plenty of time to learn all we need to know about each other. Don't feel rushed to hand me all of your secrets now. Let me earn that trust. I'm okay with that."

"Oh." Emotion twisted in her stomach. He was such a good man. "That sounds reasonable, and no, I won't tell you all of my secrets for a long while, but this one... this one, you need to know. I won't feel comfortable moving forward unless you know." And she wanted to move forward. Wanted to see, like he'd said, where this interest and attraction could lead.

"Then tell me," he said. "Just blurt it out and I'll take it from there."

"You will, huh? I don't think it will be quite that simple."

"Try me."

Silly, perhaps, but she felt as if she stood on the edge of an abyss, and that speaking these words would either send her tumbling or give her wings, but that if she remained silent and kept those words bottled up, she might not fall, but she wouldn't fly, either.

Without thought, her hand went to her right breast—her reconstructed breast—and she closed her eyes, breathed and said, "In my late twenties, my gynecologist found a lump on my breast during my yearly exam. Within two weeks of that appointment—" she opened her eyes "—I was diagnosed with inflammatory breast cancer, Stage 3B, and honestly, my prognosis wasn't positive. They told me that right off, that it would be a fight. And it was."

Shock whitened Parker's complexion as her words, the meaning of them, took hold. She kept her mouth shut, waiting to see what he would say before offering any additional explanation. If he instantly bolted, she wouldn't need to say anything else. He wouldn't need to know anything more. Right now, whatever happened next was all on him.

"IBC," he said after a minute of complete silence. "Same as Bridget."

"Oh. I…didn't know." How would she? Somehow, though, she wasn't surprised, either. "I'm sorry, Parker. For that and for dumping this on you."

If his wife had suffered from the same type of breast cancer that Nicole had, he already knew all of the grisly details. Which could be good or bad. Less for her to explain. More for him to remember, to think about, worry about. Inflammatory breast cancer tended to be aggressive, and for most women, by the time it was diagnosed, had already reached Stage 3 or Stage 4.

She guessed that was the case for Parker's wife, and that Bridget's body had already started to succumb to the disease when she was diagnosed. Speculation, of course, based on all that Nicole knew from her personal experience, her doctors, the internet and the women she'd met while going through her various stages of treatment. Bonds were formed with perfect strangers when you were fighting for the same goal: getting healthy and staying alive.

Nicole's heart ramped to high speed and her stomach churned while she waited through the silence for Parker to say more. To do whatever it was he was going to do. Maybe she shouldn't have told him so quickly, but she couldn't date the man without letting him in, without providing information that would—despite how painful and scary—offer both of them protection in the future. He had to know, and she needed him to know, before they took another step. That didn't change how awful the situation was. On either side.

Parker leaned forward, resting his elbows on his knees and his forehead in his hands, and a visible shudder rippled through his muscular arms, the lean span of his back, his long, denim-covered legs. She hurt for him, for whatever memories and thoughts were circling through his brain. But she hurt for herself, too, for her own memories and thoughts, her own fears and vulnerabilities. He would bolt. Of course he would. She wouldn't even blame him for doing so.

As if he'd read her mind, he abruptly stood, and she believed with every fiber of her being that his goal was to collect his girls, offer a few kind words and get out of her house as fast as those long legs could manage. Why wouldn't he? He'd gone through hell once. For a woman he loved, had cherished, had planned on spending his entire life with.

Why would he—why would *anyone*—take that chance for a woman he barely knew? Didn't matter she was healthy today. The statistics, which he would know as well as she did, proved that she was at greater risk for a recurrence than other women were for a first occurrence. He would view her as a ticking bomb, and she couldn't imagine how he'd consider putting himself or his daughters through the explosion and aftermath a second time.

"Nicole," he said, his voice rough and uneven. "I am so sorry."

"I know. I understand, I do, and it's okay." She lifted her shoulders and went for a confident, don't-worry-about-me type of smile. "You don't have to explain or—"

"Explain?" he asked, walking to her. "Explain why I wish you'd bought a sofa, so I could sit next to you and hold you? Or that I'm sorry or that I wish you'd never even heard of this disease, let alone had to fight it in your twenties?"

"I...I..." What was happening here? Why wasn't he rushing to her bedroom to get his daughters? Why wasn't he halfway out the door by now? And then, her traitorous body, all that pent-up fear and exhaustion from the past, won the war on her bravery, and she started to cry. Not loud, gasping tears. But tears, just the same. "I'm sorry. I'm okay."

He pulled her up and into his arms, without a moment's hesitation, and held her so close, so tight, and darn if her tears didn't fall faster. Harder. "Go ahead and cry. I got you."

"Stupid to cry," she mumbled into his shirt, her words drenched with tears. "That w-was over four years ago. I'm healthy now. I don't know why I'm c-crying."

"Because it's a painful memory that you probably don't talk about often, and you just shared part of that experience with me. Makes total sense." Turning them around, his arms still holding her tight, he pulled her onto his lap as he sat down in a chair. "Thank you for telling me, Nicole. You didn't have to. You could've kept this to yourself. I'm glad you chose to share."

"You needed to know," she said, her voice stronger. "Wasn't fair not to tell you."

"Fair doesn't come into the equation," he said quietly, his hand stroking her back in small, even circles. "This is your story, a huge piece of what makes you, you. Those pieces are valuable. I'm honored you wanted to let me in, that you cared enough to do so."

Another round of silence fell, but it wasn't uncomfortable or thick. There was an ease between them, a naturalness that defied reason. Strength and comfort, security and warmth. A reality she'd never really known with another person. Yet another miracle? She thought so.

Even if the potential for more had disappeared. As he'd said earlier: Friendships were good. Good friendships were better. And with this man, she sensed a best friend in the making.

Chapter Seven

Paul and Margaret Foster's home was a cacophony of sound, scents and activity when Parker, Erin and Megan arrived on Thanksgiving Day. The Foster family had been large to begin with, but with all the kids married now, and half of them with children of various ages, there were a lot of people celebrating the day together. All told, they were a group of seventeen.

Reid, Daisy and the twins were in attendance, naturally. Cole, the youngest of the Foster brothers, was there with his wife, Rachel. Next in line was Dylan, his wife, Chelsea, and their children: six-year-old Henry and two-month-old Hazel. Bringing the number to seventeen—counting Parker and the girls—was Haley, the youngest of the siblings, and her husband, Gavin.

And not only were the Fosters close, they were also a

handsome family. Reid and Cole took after their father, with dark, almost-black hair and brown eyes, while Dylan and Haley were blessed with Margaret's hazel-green eyes and auburn hair. Good genetics, from the inside out. People who knew what mattered in life. Parker was grateful to every one of them.

The second he walked in, the girls evaporated into the Foster clan, at home here as much as they were in their own house or when they were at Daisy and Reid's place. Parker had almost grown up in this house, himself, as he and Reid had met in grade school and forged a friendship that hadn't only endured, it had strengthened. In Parker's mind, Reid was his brother well before he and Daisy tied the knot. Which made the entire Foster family his, as well.

It was a good feeling, having that bond. Parker didn't see his parents very often anymore, as they had relocated to Florida to live out their retirement years. But he always had this family. Before Daisy had made it here to care for the girls, in those dark days that Parker was stuck in the hospital, Reid had stepped in to pick up the reins.

Yes. This was family, regardless of blood.

Before searching out his best friend, Parker stopped in the kitchen to drop off the pies he'd bought from a local bakery. Paul and Margaret were there, dancing around one another as they finished preparations for Thanksgiving dinner. Rachel and Haley were there, too, stepping in to help as Margaret shouted out commands like a drill sergeant. A smile wreathed itself across Parker's face as he recalled many other similar moments in this very same kitchen.

"Hello, Fosters," he said, adding his two pies to the four already decorating the table. "And Happy Thanksgiving. Looks busy in here, and everything smells delicious."

Paul grinned and winked. "You know how it goes when my wife is in charge."

"Hush, you, and finish peeling those potatoes," Margaret said. She gave Parker a quick hug and a kiss on his cheek. "Happy Thanksgiving to you, sweetie. Where are the girls?"

"Oh, they were off and running the second we stepped through the door," he said, again feeling that warm rush of family love and acceptance. "So, what can I do to help? Point me in the right direction and put me to work. Or tell me to get out of the way, if helping is more nuisance."

"Nuisance." Haley, with her long hair swept on top of her head, pointed toward the living room. "We love you, Parker, but there are already too many bodies in here. Reid was looking for you earlier. Go find him, and if you come across my husband, tell him we left the cranberry sauce at home, and he has about two hours left before dinner."

"Yeah, son," Paul said. "Save yourself."

"Those potatoes done yet?" Margaret asked good-naturedly, swatting her husband with a dish towel. "I see they're not, which means you're talking more than you're working."

"Woman," he said, pulling her in for a kiss, "you're lucky you're the love of my life."

"Yes, I am," she said without hesitation, taking a few steps back and putting her hands on her hips. "And you're mine, but neither has a thing to do with getting those potatoes done."

"Oh, they have plenty to do with the reason I'm in here with you, rather than with my sons watching the game." Paul gave her another kiss, this one on her nose, before returning to his potato-peeling task. "Don't you worry, they'll get done, and in time for dinner."

Watching the scene in front of him, Parker saw about as perfect a relationship as one could hope to have after being together for so long. It was what he had hoped for with Bridget, what he thought they would someday attain, with all those intertwining years between them filled with life, he supposed, serving as a foundation. But Bridget was gone now.

As he left the kitchen in search of Reid, a weight comprised of sadness and shock dropped squarely onto his heart. How was it that the first woman to inspire that hope since Bridget's death had almost died from the same disease? It seemed impossible. About as impossible as how he'd come across Roscoe that night, yet both were true.

Both had happened.

In the living room, the game played on the flat screen, but the sound was muted. Reid sat in the center of the floor, one twin on each knee, while he attempted to read them a book. Charlotte kept trying to turn the pages in quick succession, while Alexander was busy laughing at Gavin and Cole, both of whom sat on the couch making funny faces at the boy. Dylan was in one of the armchairs, paying rapt attention to the game, but he smiled as Parker entered and waved his hand in greeting. On the other side of the room, Daisy, Megan and Henry—Dylan and Chelsea's son—were building with Legos.

He didn't see Erin, Chelsea or baby Hazel, but guessed they were all together. Erin adored Hazel, and she liked being around Chelsea.

Well, she enjoyed being around all of her aunts, as well as Margaret. Loving women who had taken both his girls under their wings to offer them the type of guidance and affection they didn't have without Bridget. As Erin grew older, she seemed more acutely aware of that loss, and he assumed the same would happen with Megan. So yeah, he was grateful to Daisy and Chelsea, Rachel, Haley and Margaret, but no one could ever fully replace Bridget's role.

There was simply nothing he could do about that. And Nicole's admission had startled him, through and through. He'd thought of little else since, and he'd meant to stop by, talk to her more this past week, but with the holiday, work had been busier than normal. They had texted each day, though, and again this morning. Just nothing of significance.

He'd have to rectify that soon. Her heart mattered, and he did not want her thinking that he was going to disappear because she'd fought like hell and had managed to beat the same cancer that had killed Bridget. Truth was, he was proud of her strength.

But he had concerns, some valid and some not so much. Hell. He could get hit by a semi on his way to work, or slip and fall in the shower and crack open his skull. The fact she'd once had breast cancer, that she could get it again, shouldn't hold any more weight than the skiing accident that could've made his daughters orphans. Yet somehow, he felt the weight.

Sighing, he sat next to Reid and tickled Charlotte's arm. "Sorry to say, but neither of your children seem all that interested in this book," he said to Reid. "Going to have to up your game."

With a raised brow, Reid said, "That is entirely unhelpful. What would you suggest?"

"Different voices, inflections." Parker grinned. "The girls used to like dressing me in different hats, or throwing a scarf around my neck, depending on the book and the character. We still have an entire box of reading accoutrements. Hats, scarves, sunglasses."

It was sad, actually, how that had stopped. Not all that long ago, either. Maybe a year.

"Daisy reads to them and they are enthralled," Reid said, giving up and letting the kids off his lap. Alexander went to Cole and Gavin, instantly, while Charlotte made a beeline for her mother. "I read to them and bore them in seconds. Wouldn't be so bad if they fell asleep."

"Tell ya what. I'll do you a huge favor and bring over the reading accessories." Parker lightly punched Reid's arm. "You don't owe me a thing, either. Just carry on the tradition."

"Sure. Why not? I'll give anything a try." Reid's

dark eyes narrowed when he finally looked at Parker. "You and the girls okay? Anything going on?"

"Stop with your mother's mind reading trick," Parker said after a momentary pause. "I'm fine. The girls are fine. Just a long few weeks with a lot going on. I'm tired."

"Nah. There's something else." Rising to his feet, Reid crossed the room to his wife, said something Parker couldn't hear and then returned. "Get up. Let's go for a walk. I've been meaning to talk to you about something, anyway. Might as well do it now."

Following suit, Parker stood. "If you need to talk, that's cool. Me, though? I'm good."

"Yup. Sure you are."

They grabbed their coats and went outside, through the back door, into a crisp and clear November afternoon. Trees surrounded the property, and over the years, trails had been forged by the Foster kids in their explorations. In silent agreement, Reid and Parker started down one of those trails, and for a few minutes, neither spoke. The fresh air invigorated Parker, let loose some of the gloom clouding his brain, and for the first time since Nicole's revelation, he relaxed.

That didn't equate to having a conversation with Reid about Bridget or Nicole, though, so before his friend could fire off a question, Parker said, "What is it you wanted to talk about?"

Pausing at a clearing, Reid said, "I'll get there, but first, are you sure there's nothing going on with you or the girls? Happy to listen if you need an ear."

"I'm good. They're good. Told you that earlier." Reid

was like a dog with a bone, though, and Parker didn't think he'd let up unless he told him something. Anything. "I've met someone, but it's early days. As in, so early we haven't had an official date yet."

Reid took in the information with a grin. "Anyone I know?"

Ah. Hell. "Actually, yeah. I guess her brother, Ryan, is married to your cousin Andi."

"You're serious?" Reid's grin widened into a full-fledged smile. "I remember her. Only met her the one time, but she seemed really nice. Smart, too."

"She's both. But there isn't anything to talk about there just yet," Parker said, intending to put the conversation back on course. "So, moving on. What did you want to talk about?"

Reid leaned against a tree. "The twins' birthday is soon."

"I'm aware of my niece and nephew's birthday," Parker said, doing the same and leaning against the tree next to Reid's. "I'm guessing that isn't what you really want to tell me."

"Just stating, their birthday is next month." Reid kicked at the snow with one of his boots. "Not sure if you know this, but my dad taught us kids to ski early. We were barely walking when he started. I'd like to do the same with Charlotte and Alexander. Obviously, nothing extreme."

Seeing how the Fosters were raised on the slopes, and that Reid's job was as a ski patroller, his decision to teach his kids to ski didn't come as a surprise. Nor did the fact that he wanted to start them young. Parker understood the benefits well enough. They'd learn easier now, find an element of comfort rather than fear at the idea and have a lot of fun.

What he didn't understand was why Reid had brought him into this decision, unless... Hmm. "Does Daisy have an issue with the idea?"

"Nope. She's on board, if a little nervous." Reid shrugged. "She trusts me, knows I would never put our kids in harm's way. She isn't the reason for this conversation. I was hoping you'd give me a hand in teaching them. You're an excellent skier. My kids love and trust you, and you're a dad, so you'll be more aware of what they need than, say, Cole or Gavin."

Whoa. "I haven't been on a pair of skis since my accident. Three years ago."

"I know that, too. I remember the accident, Parker." As he shook his head, Reid's gaze grew hooded. "I found you. I won't forget that moment any easier than you will."

"Then you have to know I'm not the best candidate. Cole or Gavin are much better choices, and they're both great with kids." Hell, Gavin ran a camp for foster kids. "Haley. Your dad. You have plenty of able and skilled family members to choose from. Why me?"

"Ever hear of the expression 'Get back on the horse'?"

It was Parker's turn to kick at the snow. "Of course I have. Doesn't apply here. I don't ski anymore, made that decision after the accident, and that isn't changing."

"Not asking you to do anything more than help me at the bunny hill," Reid pointed out, his voice cool and rational. "An hour or two a week, at most. And I'm not assuming you'll want to stay after and ski with me down a black run, or even a blue. The bunny hill, Parker."

For skiers, a blue run meant an intermediate skill level, while black meant advanced. They used to run both together, regularly. There were a ton of good memories there, hours spent on the slopes, hanging with Reid and often Cole and Dylan. Good times. They'd had a lot of them, no doubt. But those days were long gone, and no, Parker had no desire to ever ski either type of run again. Or to ski, period. He didn't miss or need the sport.

But his girls? They needed *him*. He was their last parent. All they had left.

"I can't believe you're asking this," he said. "You know it isn't about the bunny hill, or teaching the kids. I adore Charlotte and Alexander. I'd do just about anything for them."

"Then do this," Reid said, in that same logical tone. "I'd appreciate your help. We're talking the bunny hill, Parker. Chances are high we won't even get that far the first day."

"It isn't about the bunny hill," Parker repeated. "The bunny hill isn't the issue."

"I know that, too. The issue is fear."

Yeah, well, he couldn't argue with Reid's assessment. "So what if it is? Fear can be healthy. Helps you see where the boundaries in life are. And this is a boundary I don't intend on crossing." Tension hardened his jaw, his shoulders. "I appreciate that you trust me enough to ask, but I need you to understand why I can't. Respect this boundary, please."

With a sharp nod that resonated of disappointment, Reid said, "Can't promise I won't bring it up again, but your choices remain yours, and I do respect them. Do me a favor, though, and give it some more thought. Let the idea sink in a bit and see where it lands."

Agreeing to even consider the idea further rankled, but this man was his best friend. Had stepped in to care for his daughters while Parker couldn't. He was Daisy's husband. The way Parker saw it, he didn't have much other choice but to say, "I can do that."

Reid gave Parker a brotherly slap on the shoulder. "Thanks."

"For allowing you to guilt me into thinking about something I'd rather not?" Parker asked with a short laugh. "You're welcome? I guess? Does Daisy ever win an argument with you?"

"She does," Reid affirmed. "More often than not, actually. And I didn't win here, either, now, did I? You've said no, which is not the response I was aiming for. That being said, it's Thanksgiving. Everyone we love is in that house, safe and happy and healthy."

True statement there.

"Let's get back to them, then," Parker said, suddenly remembering Haley's request. "Your sister asked me to tell Gavin he needs to go home and get the cranberry sauce, which I promptly forgot until this minute. Don't want to ruin Thanksgiving."

"Yeah, we better tell him posthaste." Reid pushed himself off the tree and, as they started toward the house, said in an almost-casual tone, "In addition to what you said about boundaries, fear can also stop you from experiencing all that life has to offer. It's a fine line."

And that was another statement that resonated as true.

Parker sighed, nodded and admitted to himself that he'd have to think about that some, see where it fell in with the rest. Not only about teaching the twins to ski, but about Nicole. About her history and his. And if the weight he felt had substance, was a boundary he should pay attention to, or if it was nothing more than a hurdle to jump and leave behind.

By early Thanksgiving evening, the Bradshaw household was winding down from a marathon day of cooking, eating, card playing and a quickly thrown-together outing that consisted of touch football and a snowman building contest. Nicole was overstuffed, but happy.

She adored her family, including her new sister-in-law, Andi.

Andrea Caputo had entered her brother's life as a client. Ryan worked as a physical therapist, and Andi had needed help recovering after a traumatic incident in the hospital where she'd worked in Rhode Island. They had connected, fallen in love and tied the knot.

She couldn't be happier for her brother. He had chosen well. Though, to hear him talk, he said there wasn't any choice involved. Andi had shown up one day, his instincts had demanded she was the one meant for him, she felt the same and it was a done deal. There were no alternatives. Of course, the doing wasn't quite that simple. They were human and made mistakes, as humans are apt to do, and it took them a bit to unravel the complexities to find their happily-ever-after. But the instinct that Ryan spoke of was what really resonated for Nicole.

Anything good took work. Anything worthwhile held risk. And if you wanted something to last, you had to put in the work and accept the risk and then work some more. Having the courage to proceed, without any guarantees for a good outcome. She understood and believed in this, through and through. Had applied that very same concept to many areas of her life, including her recovery, and now, trying to become a mother.

But with love, it was the *knowing* when to risk it all that eluded her.

Ryan and their father, Jerry, were half out of it in the living room, dozing in the La-Z-Boy chairs in front of the television, while their mother, Brenda, and Andi were playing another card game in the dining room. Nicole had just finished tidying the kitchen for her mother's benefit, since Brenda had done most of the cooking that day. She figured if she wanted some one-on-one time with Ryan, this was the best chance she was going to get.

She tapped him on his shoulder, and when that didn't work, she tugged his short, dark brown hair. He opened one eye, and then the other. "Hmm. What's up, Nic?"

"Wake up and take a walk with me? Please?"

"Seriously? How can you want to take a walk?" Ryan asked. "Aren't you exhausted?"

"I…need some brother time," she admitted softly. "So, walk with me?"

That was all it took. Standing, he stretched his arms above his head and yawned. "Sure thing. But if it's conversation you want, can we sneak off to the back porch and skip the walk?"

"That works for me," she said. "I'll even bring the coffee."

Jerry and Brenda Bradshaw had updated this house from top to bottom when they bought it, and in the doing, had insulated the walls that surrounded the sunporch. While the room wasn't actually heated, the insulation, storm windows and a couple of space heaters kept the area fairly comfortable, even in the winter. Except for those subzero days, which today wasn't, fortunately.

She found Ryan in one of the chairs, arms crooked behind his head, with a lazy and content smile playing over his face. Setting his coffee mug on the end table, she sat across from him. "It's been a good day. I'm glad you and Andi decided to celebrate Thanksgiving here."

"We visited her family last week, and we'll be there over Christmas," Ryan said. "But we'll find time to be together, I'm sure. Maybe when we get back? If that works for you?"

"Before or after, Ryan. Won't feel like Christmas without you." Nicole sipped her coffee. How to say what she wanted without making it too obvious? "You're happy, right? With Andi?"

"Very," he said. "What makes you ask?"

"Oh," she said lightly, "just checking in. Sisters tend to do that."

"Uh-huh. There's more to this, I'm sure. Spill."

Nicole cupped her hands around the mug and breathed in the warmth. This was Ryan. She could ask him anything, anytime. "You told me once that when you first met Andi, you knew she was who you'd been waiting for. You meant when you first met, as in literally, right? Not after a date or a kiss or even a cup of coffee, but within minutes of seeing her?"

"More like seconds." Ryan tipped his head to the side, his attention fully on Nicole. "Don't get me wrong, I didn't instantly trust that knowing, but yeah, I can look back now, see it for what it was and know it was there." He shrugged. "Does that make sense?"

"Maybe." Nicole rolled her bottom lip into her mouth. "How did you…um…know?"

"Heavy question," Ryan said. "Seems important."

"It is."

"Wish I had a clear answer for you, sis," Ryan said. "I don't. All I can tell you is that something clicked inside, and there was this knowledge that wasn't there before. The sun shone brighter. The air smelled sweeter. Coffee—" he raised his cup "—tasted better."

"Rather poetic, huh?" she teased. "You loved her like a love song?"

"Pretty much, yeah," he said, with zero embarrassment coloring his tenor. "Love songs are written for a reason. I don't know if any of what I've said helps, but

I am guessing you've met someone? And this someone is why you're asking these questions?"

"I have," she admitted softly. "But it's complex and...let's just go with complex."

"It always is." Leaning forward, Ryan patted Nicole's knee, as if they were kids again and he'd found her holed up somewhere, crying. "Trust your heart. Best advice I got."

"What if there are more hearts on the line than just two?"

Took her brother a second to connect the dots, but when he did, he said, "Ah. Kids are involved. That makes it tougher, but my advice holds." He paused a beat, swallowed a gulp of coffee. Then, "You have a good heart, Nic. I don't believe it will lead you wrong."

"It's complex," she repeated. "Thank you, though."

He nodded, smiled. "Whatever you need, I'm here for you. Nothing changes that."

"I know," she said. "Same goes for me—I'm here for you."

They sat for a few minutes then, not speaking, just drinking their coffee. Before they went back inside, Ryan said, "Everything else is good for you? Nothing I should worry about, healthwise? No news on the maybe-a-baby front? Just the same old, same old?"

Nicole put her hand on her stomach. She hadn't taken that test yet, and she had decided to wait it out another week, at least, if not another two. "Healthy, strong, and no, no news yet."

"Well. Keep me informed. I'm looking forward to uncle duty." Ryan gave her a quick hug. "I'm proud of you, for going after what you want. And as far as this mystery man goes? He'd be lucky to have you in his life. Never doubt that, okay?"

"I know my worth," she said. "But I know his, too. And this entire situation is—"

"Complex," Ryan said, finishing her sentence. "Aren't all relationships, though?"

"With humans? Yeah. Why do you think I love Roscoe so much? Easiest relationship in my life." Except, of course, when he ran away and frightened her half to death. "Hey. Thanks for waking from your nap to talk. It…means a lot to me, Ryan."

"What else are brothers for?"

They walked inside, finding the rest of their family exactly where they left them. Nicole stayed another half an hour before going home. Roscoe would need to go out, and she wanted a long, hot bubble bath. Also, she had an inkling she might hear from Parker.

And she'd rather be alone if that inkling proved correct. Which it did, about two hours later, with a text that read:

Hope your day was fantastic! My sister is keeping the girls overnight on Saturday. Was thinking we could go out to dinner or something. You in?

She texted back, Sure! Sardine pizza?

Ah. No, he replied. I have something more interesting in mind. But you'll have to trust me, and not ask for any details. Deal?

She agreed, and later, while she soaked in the tub,

she wondered if this was a date or an outing between friends. If he'd called, rather than texted, she'd have a better idea. As it was, she'd have to wait to see. Either way, she would listen to Ryan's advice and trust in her heart.

Chapter Eight

"Come on, girls," Parker hollered up the stairs the following Saturday, a mere thirty minutes before he was supposed to pick up Nicole. First, he had to drop off Erin and Megan at Daisy and Reid's, and they were running behind schedule. "We need to get going."

The girls ran down the stairs carrying their overnight bags. Megan was excited, but Erin had dragged her feet for the past hour. And she'd been quieter than normal, even more introspective, for the past week. Something was going on with his eldest daughter; Parker just wasn't sure what. He'd tried to talk with her, but she swore she was fine.

Maybe she was. He could be reading far too much into the relatively small change in her demeanor. But if there was something bothering her, either she'd tell him what was on her mind or he'd figure it out. Eventually. Erin wouldn't be rushed. The kid lived in her head more often than not, just as Parker's sister did. The two were a lot alike, in looks and in personality.

Once they were at Daisy's, he pulled his sister aside and asked her to see if she could get Erin to open up, and explained why. His sister agreed, told him not to worry and almost shoved him out of her front door with the order to relax and enjoy himself.

Well, that was the plan.

Even so, his palms were sweaty when he rang Nicole's doorbell. He might as well have jumped into a time warp and returned to his sixteen-year-old self, his nerves were that jittery. That had to be good, really. If he wasn't nervous, he'd have to question why he'd asked Nicole out in the first place. A first date with a woman should induce anxiety, to a certain extent.

And when she opened the door, his heart could've been a balloon, the way it seemed to blow up in his chest. She looked... *Beautiful* didn't come close to being an accurate enough description. Her pale blond hair was twisted into a loose knot on the back of her head, with a few tendrils framing her face. Those green-gold eyes were outlined in smoky gray, and her lips were a glossy rosy pink. Not too dark. Not too light. Just perfect.

No, *beautiful* didn't quite cut it. *Ethereal* came to mind. As did *delicate* and *alluring*.

Elegant, too, even in a pair of black jeans and a soft, almost-fuzzy jade green sweater that fell slightly off one shoulder. Lord, he was a lucky man to have this woman on his arm.

"You look…beautiful, Nicole," he said, falling back on the only word he felt comfortable using. He couldn't tell her she looked ethereal or delicate, now, could he? "Simply beautiful."

There was that blush again, washing over her pale, creamy skin. She put on her coat and stepped outside, locking the door behind her. He'd left his coat in the car. He was too sweaty to put on another layer. Too nervous and too filled with anticipation.

"Thank you, Parker. You look pretty good, yourself," she said, the smallest of tremors perceptible in her speech. Meant she was nervous, too, and Parker decided that was also an excellent sign. Reaching over, she tapped the front of his shirt. "Whatever color of blue this is suits you. Brings out the blue in your eyes."

Was that warmth drenching his cheeks? Was *he* blushing? Had he now become a sixteen-year-old girl? "Thank you. And I don't know. I just call it dark blue." He did not mention how long it had taken to choose which shirt, which pair of jeans, he should wear. Longer than it should've, he knew that. "Ready?"

"Well, that's just it," she said as he opened the car door for her, "I don't know what we're doing, so how can I know if I'm ready or not? You're not expecting me to jump out of a plane or anything, are you? Because that—" she buckled her seat belt "—I am not ready for."

"Skydiving is not on the agenda. I can promise you that." Damn if his palms weren't still sweating. They'd have to stop, or he wouldn't be able to hold her hand all night. And at some point, he really, really wanted to hold her hand. "Food is involved," he said, once he was settled in the car, "but not at an actual restaurant. We'll be working for our dinner."

"Working, huh?"

"Yep. But I think we'll have fun."

More important than merely having fun, though, he hoped spending time together tonight lifted the weight he'd carried around since learning of her battle with cancer. And he hoped the fear would dissipate, so he could focus 100 percent on the rational, positive facts: he liked this woman. A lot. He saw potential here. Also, a lot. He wanted to embrace the good—hell, the amazing—possibilities, rather than dwell on the negative. That was the choice he'd made, what he wanted to bring up later, but he'd like to send this specific demon running.

"There is no think, only do," she said, in a better than acceptable Yoda impersonation. "And yes, I am fully aware that quote isn't accurate, but in this case, it fits."

Ah. The woman quoted from *Star Wars*. Yeah, he was a goner.

Close to four hours later, Parker and Nicole were seated at a candlelit table, enjoying a romantic meal that consisted of a panzanella salad, risotto with Italian ham and peas, chicken scaloppini and a luscious chocolate amaretto cake for dessert. The catch was that they'd made the meal together, at a couples cooking class for their first date.

And it *was* a date. She no longer held any confusion about Parker's intentions for the night. She couldn't deny the ingenuity of his plan, either, or the fun they'd had while the instructor walked them through each portion of the meal. Oh, some of the steps were already done for them, or it would've taken longer than three hours to prepare and cook the entire meal, but they were left mostly in charge, and they'd worked as a team.

They chatted about their individual Thanksgivings and families, laughed at their spills and other mishaps as they cooked, and all of it, from beginning to end, had flowed effortlessly. Her mother, if Brenda had been here to see them, would've called them two peas in a pod, or a match made in heaven, or something else along those lines. And despite the complexities involved in moving forward with a possible relationship, Nicole would agree.

Because in addition to the great teamwork, a natural effervescence sparkled between them. It was always there, lingering. And when their hands brushed, their hips touched, he smiled and she laughed, that constant sizzle of want, desire, *need*, heightened and pulsed and expanded, until it just about sucked every bit of oxygen from the room. Until the only images in her mind were that of touching him, kissing him and being touched and kissed in return.

For hours on end. Days. Weeks. *Forever.*

Throughout the evening, she continually had to

pummel those images into submission and tuck them into a corner, otherwise she feared she might actually act on them by putting her hands on his shoulders and her lips on his lips, and, well, this was the beginning of their *first* date. They had more to talk about. More time to spend together. Just more *them* before anything else could or should occur. And there was the not-so-little fact that she might be pregnant.

A possibility she hadn't mentioned as of yet. She would tell him about her attempts and her reasons for them, whether she was pregnant or not, but she'd decided to hold off until she knew one way or the other. How she broached that particular conversation, the context itself, would vary depending on if she was or wasn't. Another week or two, and she'd know, and she'd tackle the topic. Because if she wasn't pregnant, and she and Parker were dating, she'd have to think about what to do next. If she chose to continue her attempts, he'd have to know.

"You suddenly got quiet," Parker said, interrupting her thoughts. "Don't tell me I've worn you out already, because that would be a shame. I've more on the agenda for tonight."

That statement, combined with her *kissing* and *touching* images, reignited her desire, her want for this man, and to help quell the fire, she swallowed a large mouthful of ice water. "More on the agenda?" she asked, setting her glass on the table. "I can't imagine what will top this, but I can't wait to see what you have planned. Feel like passing on a clue or two?"

A quirky grin appeared. "Not really. I rather like

surprising you. Hope you're okay with surprises, because I don't think that is likely to change."

"Oh, I don't mind surprises, so long as they are good ones."

"Only good for you. It's what you deserve." His jaw clamped shut after he spoke the words, as if he'd just surprised himself. Then, "I'm having a great time, Nicole. You're a remarkable woman and, as odd as this sounds, I'm glad I almost ran you over with my car. Gladder I didn't actually run you over, but you know what I mean."

"I do, and...Parker, you're the remarkable one. I'm just...me."

"Right. That's what I said. Remarkable."

The compliment lit her from the inside out, as surely as the candles made the table glow. This man was special. Unique. As was the connection growing between them.

"Thank you. I'm happy to know you, too." She wanted to say more, thought maybe she should, even, but in the end, she chose not to. Rather, she leaned against her chair and sighed. "I ate all day on Thanksgiving, a mere forty-eight hours ago, and now, this meal. It will be weeks before I work off the extra calories. If my jeans don't fit tomorrow, I'm blaming you."

Holding up his hands, as if in surrender, he chuckled. "That's fine. I'll take the blame. What I want to know," he said, pushing his dinner plate to the side, "is if that means you're not interested in dessert, and I have to eat this entire cake by myself. Don't make me do it, Nicole."

"By entire, you mean this six-inch mini cake?" she teased. "Pretty sure you won't have a problem finishing that off, but no, I'm a sucker for punishment. And I love my chocolate."

"A sucker for punishment? That's good news." With a wink and a smile, he said, "Because I like a woman who...doesn't refuse dessert."

"Then you'll love me, because I...um...that is, I never refuse dessert."

His gaze found and locked onto hers, and that telltale shiver wove its way through her body. Because of a look. Just one look. He kept that gaze on her as he pushed his chair around the table, so they were seated side by side, so close their thighs touched. Putting the unsliced cake in front of them, he handed her a fork, saying, "Then dig in. Plates are for amateurs."

She didn't verbally respond, just broke off a chunk of the scrumptiously rich cake with her fork and popped it in her mouth. An unbidden moan escaped at the taste, the way the confection melted on her tongue and slipped down her throat. Sighing in pleasure, she went for a second bite before realizing how she must have looked, how she must have sounded.

"Wow," she said, putting down her fork. "That might be the best cake I've ever had."

"Me, too," he said, his eyes a dark and stormy shade of blue. And they were focused on her mouth, her lips, her throat. "Delicious. Delectable. Perfection."

"Your fork is clean," she said as another shiver trembled through her, as her skin warmed beneath the hunger so evident in Parker's gaze. "You can't say that until you actually taste the…cake."

"But I can. I did." Closing his eyes, he drew in a ragged-sounding breath. When he opened them again, he said, "But you're right, I should try the cake."

Still, he didn't move to do so, just kept looking at her, and she had to fight hard not to give in to that bone-deep attraction, the temptation, the driving *instinct* to trail her fingers along his jaw, his cheek, and into his hair. She had to fight not to push her mouth against his, claim him as hers and offer herself as his, because yes, that was what she felt. That they fit. Together.

Meant to be. Supposed to be.

Instead, since giving in to any of that would certainly be rule number one of what not to do on a first date, she broke off another chunk of cake. "Here," she said, touching his lips with the fork. "Taste this. I promise it will be the best chocolate cake you've ever had."

She saw him swallow before he even opened his mouth. She saw the hunger ramp even higher in his gaze. She saw his jaw flinch and his shoulders shake. These signs told her that she was getting to him just as deeply, just as surely as he was getting to her. And she liked having this knowledge. It seemed to strengthen all she'd felt from the first moment they'd met.

Opening his mouth, he ate the bite of cake she offered, but other than that slight, barely there movement, he didn't budge an inch. Every part of him remained firmly focused on her, on the heat that saturated the air, on the silent acknowledgment that they were on the same page.

"Delicious. Delectable," he said again. "Perfection. Just like you."

That final word served to shake her from the moment. "I'm not perfect, Parker."

"No one is, but have you considered… Well, probably too soon to say that."

"Say what you're thinking. Say what you need."

"You're sure? Because I prefer it that way," he said, his tone serious. "I'm not the type of guy to beat around the bush or play word games, but I don't want you to misunderstand, either."

Oh. He was going to jump in headfirst, was he? That was good. Probably, that was good. Scary, too, though. Trusting her gut, she said, "Most of the time, I'm the same. So yes, I'm sure."

Removing the fork from her grasp, he set it on the table and then captured her hand with his. He held it tightly, securely. "No, you're not perfect. I'm not, either. No one is," he repeated with a short, almost-under-his-breath laugh. "Perhaps, though, we're perfect for each other. Don't worry, I'm not saying we *are*, and we have a way to go before determining that, but the possibility exists. I feel it. Pretty sure you feel it, too, but…uh… let me know if I'm wrong."

"You're not wrong." She breathed the words more than she spoke them. "But, Parker, there is a lot here that we'll eventually need to discuss. Things I haven't told you yet, that I'm not ready to tell you, and I'm guessing you have concerns. I mean, the girls...their mom."

"Okay, let's tackle some of this now," Parker said after a moment's pause. "Because yes, of course there are concerns. I'm not going to lie. I've carried this weight of...I don't know how to describe it...foreboding, I guess, ever since you told me you had IBC. It's scary."

"I live with that foreboding," she said, putting truth to what she barely admitted to herself most days. "And I won't lie, either. It's difficult, knowing that just because I beat it once, just because I've been healthy for four years, doesn't mean the cancer won't come back. In the weeks before I see my oncologist, I am awash with fear that the tide will change again."

"I can imagine," Parker said, still holding on to her hand. She liked that, too, that he hadn't let go. "And I would have the same fear, right alongside you, which is part of the foreboding, I suppose. I've gone through this, from beginning to end, and..." He trailed off as his voice broke. A few seconds passed while he regained his composure. Then, "The disease annihilated Bridget, and I don't solely mean because she died. I mean with what it did to her. Physically. Mentally. Emotionally. And there wasn't a damn thing I could do to fix any of it."

"That's scary, thinking about going through it all again, if we were together and—"

"It is, Nicole. I failed Bridget. Walking into another scenario where there is absolutely nothing I can do to change the outcome...it hasn't been easy to consider."

On some level, Nicole had known all of this. But to

hear the devastation in his voice, to see it in his eyes, brought the knowledge into crystal clear perspective. Along with the crippling loss, along with raising his daughters without their mother, he believed he somehow failed Bridget. She understood. And oh, she felt for him, wished she had the words to ease his pain.

She didn't, though. The first words she thought of, he already knew and had likely heard time and again. From his sister. His friends. At one point, probably even from Bridget herself. Still, she had to try. And the trying wasn't about convincing him to accept her and what might or what might not happen between them—it was about healing a wound.

Words he'd heard before wouldn't—couldn't—suddenly make a difference now, merely because they were coming from her. But if she changed the angle of the camera lens, shared the view from her eyes, her experiences, maybe…well, maybe those words would do what the others hadn't. Difficult? Yes. But she had the sense it was what he needed.

"Listen to me," she said. "Yes, your wife was dying in front of you, a little more each day, and you felt helpless. But that doesn't mean you failed. And I know this isn't quite the same, but my brother and parents went through that with me, so here's what I can tell you from my perspective." It was Nicole's turn to squeeze Parker's hand. "Every kindness, every thoughtful action my family did for me offered help and hope, security and comfort."

"I'm sure it did, and I'm relieved you had them, but that isn't what I am trying to express." Parker's frustration was evident to Nicole. In the tight manner in which he spoke, in the tension rippling through his shoulders to his arms to the hand she held. "Bringing her juice, rubbing her feet, holding her hair while she puked didn't fix *anything*."

Tears flooded her eyes, but Nicole did not let them fall. Later, she would. Later.

"No, none of that cured her cancer, but that's different from not being able to fix anything. I can promise you that you did. When my mother would sit there and paint my toenails bright red, so I had something pretty to look at, or when my brother put all of my favorite songs on my tablet, or when my father brought me a chocolate malt because I craved them constantly, those actions bolstered me, Parker. They made me stronger, so I was better able to fight."

"You survived," he said, pointing out the obvious. "She did not."

"That isn't because my family somehow helped me more than you helped Bridget," Nicole said, hoping he'd cross this chasm. See what she was so desperately trying to share. "It's the disease. My body. Her body. Every fight is different, you know that, but—" and oh, Lord, she hoped she was right with this guess "—I bet Bridget lasted longer than the doctors thought she would, which gave her more opportunity to keep fighting. Am I right?"

He blinked once. Twice. A third time before acknowledging her question with a nod. "She did. They gave her less than six months when she was diagnosed, and she survived for more than twice that." He let out a breath. "For a while, we thought…she had beat it."

Ouch. Those tears she'd just squelched—tears made up of Parker's pain—burned bright and hot and heavy behind her eyes. They'd gone through hell, Parker and Bridget, had found hope again and then watched it fade away in slow, stuttering, gasping steps.

Unfair, to be shown the sun but not allowed to stand in its rays.

"Well. Okay, then," she said, swallowing the pain as best she could. "You've proved my point, though it might be hard for you to admit, to accept. But, Parker? You played a role in that. Her meds, the chemo, her own positive attitude and the girls were all part of the reason, but so were you and everything you did to see to her comfort, to make her smile, to help her relax… Every bit of that gave her more strength than she would've had otherwise."

"That's how it was for you?" he asked. "Straight up."

"Straight up. That is how it was for me," Nicole said, speaking the God's honest truth, "and while I have no statistical data to back this up, the women I went through chemo with, the women I saw day in and day out? Those who had a solid support system…loving husbands, friends and family, well, they fared better than those who didn't."

Her words, the emotion behind them, echoed in the ensuing silence. Their hands remained clasped, fingers entwined, and she felt him relax, felt him take a deep breath and then another, and she believed, hoped, that he might have just let go some of this burden.

"Well," he said, a minute, maybe two minutes, later, "I didn't expect this conversation to go where it did, but thank you for your insight, Nicole. I have a better understanding now."

"Oh, Parker, you're so welcome. I… Usually it's hard for me to talk about any of this, but with you, it's…easier, somehow." Because of the connection between them, or because of his experience with Bridget? Both, probably. "Thank you, too, for listening."

Lightly, he kissed her on her forehead. "You're welcome. I'll listen anytime. Just say the word. And I'm sorry, too, I hadn't meant for this to get so deep, so fast. All I was attempting to do was let you in on why I carried this weight around, but that I had decided what mattered most was getting to know you more today, and not fixate on the past or the negative what-ifs."

"I decided the same," she said, pleasure rippling and bobbing its way through her. "But I wanted to give you the opportunity to talk, I guess."

"Because you're amazing and thoughtful and kind, along with beautiful and smart and—" he kissed her again, this time on her nose "—sexy. So, from where I sit, it seems we've reached the same decision, which means, you're willing to see where this leads us?"

Her stomach somersaulted. "I would like that, Parker. I mean, we're likely going to have a lot of tough discussions, but yes, I am very much interested in seeing where this leads."

"Thank God," he said. "Now, let's finish this night on a high note, shall we?"

They weren't done for the night? "Oh. I would love that, yes. What is the plan?"

Comically waggling his eyebrows, Parker said, "That, my dear, is still a surprise."

And just as if it hadn't occurred, the emotional, difficult exchange evaporated. If anything, she felt closer to him than she had before and sensed they'd started the job of building a firm foundation on which they would stand. All good. All positive. The ease from earlier in the evening swept in, along with the desire that sent her pulse skyrocketing.

When they arrived at their next destination, she initially thought he was taking her ice-skating, but as they walked into the arena, she laughed. "Bumper cars on ice? Really? I love bumper cars but haven't tried this yet. Better watch out, Parker," she said, nudging his arm with her elbow. "I am a relentless bumper car driver. You'll have a hard time getting away."

"I'm not trying to get away, Nicole." Pulling her into his arms, in front of an entire ice arena of spectators, he lowered his mouth to hers for a kiss. Lips, firm and searching, touched hers, and she melted into his embrace, into the kiss, while holding on to his arms.

Heat, delicious and delectable, consuming and satiating, crawled through her body, inch by inch by inch, until even her fingers and her toes tingled. She pressed herself tighter against him as he deepened the kiss, pushing his tongue into her mouth, tasting and teasing and exploring. And if they hadn't been in a public place, if she already knew for certain she was not pregnant, she'd be in the process of unbuttoning his shirt and unclasping his jeans.

What he did to her, the strength of her body's response to him, was new. Exciting. And truly, more profound than anything she'd ever expected to experience. Especially so quickly. Parker had seemingly arrived out of nowhere, on a cold and blistery evening, when she'd least expected to find... Well, she wouldn't say "love." Not yet. But the potential for love existed.

And even the *potential* for love counted as a miracle.

Chapter Nine

The following Monday, Parker waited for the girls in the pickup lane at the grade school, his mind drifting, as usual, to Nicole. Their date had gone better than he could have hoped for, and while that nagging weight on his heart hadn't miraculously disappeared, it didn't seem quite as prevalent, either. Hopefully, that meant he'd eventually get rid of it altogether.

He worried, though. About falling in love again, about going through the same hell he'd barely survived with Bridget. Parker did not know how to love with only half his heart, so if he took the plunge with Nicole, that would be that. No turning back.

Even if she became ill again. Even if.

But could he find even the smallest pebble of hope to bolster Nicole if they were to ever reach such a point?

She would deserve his best, just as Bridget had, and he'd turned himself inside out for her benefit. For *their* benefit. Yet, despite the strength, courage and hope he'd surrounded them with, Bridget had still died. She'd still left him and the girls.

So, did he have the strength, the courage, to face that horror again, knowing all he now knew? The answer continued to elude, but walking away from Nicole, from the potential of what they could be, wasn't the solution.

Kids began streaming out of the school. Erin and Megan were in the middle of that stream, walking side by side, aiming toward the car, both with stiff postures and focused expressions. As they got closer, he saw Erin's red-rimmed eyes and Megan's narrowed ones, along with each of their flushed, unhappy faces. Something was wrong.

Well, hell. What could be the problem? Parker's brain put two and two together and guessed that Nicole had probably posted the cast list for the Christmas play, since rehearsals would have to start soon. Could it be that his daughters were upset by whatever roles they'd been given? Or worse, one had been cast in the cherished role of Snow White as the Ghost of Christmas Past, leaving the other disappointed and jealous?

Reaching the car a few steps ahead of her sister, Megan jumped into the back seat and scooted to the other side so Erin could use the same door. They deposited their backpacks in between them, latched their seat belts and, in almost-perfect synchronicity, each turned their heads to look out their respective windows.

"Why, hello, my darling daughters. I hope you've had a great day at school," Parker said, putting the car into gear and moving toward the street at a snail's pace. When neither responded, he swallowed a sigh. As much as he hated their bickering, if he had to choose one over the other, he preferred that to angry silence. "My day was terrific, by the way."

Not even a sigh reached his ears.

"What happened today, girls?" he asked, trying to watch them through the rearview mirror while he drove. And still nothing. They could keep up the silent routine for a while, so he might as well get right to the hornet's nest. "Guessing this has to do with the Christmas play. Specifically, the roles you've been cast in. How am I doing so far?"

"Miss Bradshaw chose her to be Snow White!" Erin blurted in a defiant, angry tone. "I'm older, Daddy. If she was going to pick one of us, she should've picked me."

"But she didn't pick you! And you have a good part, too!"

"First of all, let's try to calm down," he said. "And what part did you get, Erin?"

"I'm the Fairy Godmother, but I'm the narrator, so I'm not even really in the play! I just stand there and talk to the audience about the play. I was supposed to be Snow White."

"No, you weren't, because she picked me, and you could at least be happy for me, Erin." And in his youngest daughter's voice, Parker heard disappointment and sadness. She adored Erin, even if they did squabble, and he figured she was genuinely hurt by her older sister's reaction. "I would be happy for you if she picked you."

"You would not!" Erin kicked the back of the front passenger seat hard enough that the impact reverberated to his position behind the wheel. "You would be just as mad."

"No, I wouldn't! You're not me, so you—"

"Hey, now," Parker said, keeping his voice and demeanor as calm as possible. "No kicking, Erin. You know better. And, girls, yelling at each other isn't the way we work out disagreements. What is the first rule we're supposed to remember, no matter how mad we are?"

"That we're family and we love each other," Megan promptly answered. "And even if we're really, really mad, we should try to keep our words and voices nice."

"Exactly right." Slowing down, and then stopping at a red light, Parker said, "Tell me, Erin, what else are we supposed to do when there's a conflict?"

"I don't care. She shouldn't be Snow White. She won't remember the lines."

"I will, too, Erin. That is mean to say, because you don't know."

"Erin? I asked you a question." The light turned green. "Please answer."

"Fine," his eldest huffed. "We're supposed to try to see the other person's view, even if we don't agree with it. And then…then talk about why we're so upset, so they understand, too."

"Good girl. So, let's start with you. Why are you so upset that Megan got the part and you didn't? Think about the real reason why, and choose your words carefully," Parker warned, wishing he'd waited until they were home to start this conversation. "No more outbursts. And, Megan, please don't interrupt. Let your sister talk, and then it will be your turn. Okay?"

"Okay, Daddy," Megan said. "I won't interrupt, even if she's wrong."

"Megan, you know that isn't what we're doing here. We're focusing on understanding, not blaming. Right now it isn't about who might be right or wrong." Parker took a left-hand turn and counted his lucky stars they were only a few minutes from the house. "Go on, Erin."

"I am this upset because...b-because I wanted the p-part more," Erin said in tear-soaked syllables. Parker's heart cracked, hearing her distress. "A lot m-more, so it h-hurts and makes me m-mad and like...like—" a gulping sob broke through "—I disappointed M-Mommy."

And there it was, the crux of the issue, even if Parker didn't yet understand why Erin had those feelings. He had to keep his own emotion tamped down, which he barely managed to do when he said, "It's hard to say if you wanted to play Snow White more than your sister. We can't measure that, sweets. What concerns me the most is why you think your mom would be disappointed you didn't get that particular role, because I know for a fact that she wouldn't be."

Finally, they were driving down their street.

"B-because she said I was the p-perfect S-Snow White, in my costume, on the l-last Halloween, before...before—" She gave up trying to talk, gave up trying to do anything but cry as hard and as fervently as a little girl with a broken heart could. It tore him to shreds.

"You can be Snow White, Erin. Stop crying, please," Megan said softly, now also in tears. "I don't want to be her anymore, okay? Please stop crying."

Parker pulled into his driveway, shifted the car into Park, turned off the ignition and, after hitting the button to unlock the doors, jumped out as if his clothes were on fire. It took longer than he liked, but he got the girls out of the car and into the house, both of them now sobbing in long, agonized wails, the tears flooding their cheeks. Why hadn't he remembered that final Halloween? Erin was correct; she'd dressed as Snow White, while Megan had been a ladybug.

Bridget had chosen their costumes, and he should have remembered. That was his job.

He sat on the couch, with Erin on one side and Megan on the other, and covered all three of them with a blanket. Arms over their shoulders, he brought them as close as possible, murmuring nonsensical words of comfort, hoping his voice would give them the security they needed. Megan's sobs slowed relatively quickly, but she kept her head burrowed into Parker's chest. Erin's tears, though, they just kept coming, and he kept holding on.

When she'd calmed enough that he thought she'd pay attention, he said, "Listen to me, sweets. There isn't any way that your mom would be disappointed, especially over the part you were given in a play. She would be proud of you. Bursting with pride, kiddo. I promise you this."

"But she thought I should be Snow White for Halloween," Erin said in between her sniffles. "And I remember how much she smiled that day. Do you remember, Daddy?"

"I do. But that was because of you, sweetheart, not because of the costume you wore."

"She can be Snow White in the play, Daddy," Megan said, lifting her head from his chest. "It's okay because I thought I wanted to be her, but I don't anymore. I decided."

"You know, Megan, that is such a kindhearted offer, but that isn't a decision we can make." That she wanted to, though, to ease her sister's turmoil, resonated as such a gracious gesture, that it told Parker he'd done okay in the parenting department. Maybe even better than okay, and in this moment, he was both a proud papa and a sad one. Different emotions for very different daughters. "We would have to talk with Nicole about a decision like that, since she is in charge of the play, and it might not be what Erin really needs."

"I don't." Erin sat up and dried her tears with the back of her hand. "Now that Daddy explained, I'm okay being the Fairy Godmother, Megan," she said, her cadence still shaky, but without the desolation from earlier. *Thank God.* "She gets to wear a pretty dress, too, and I have lots more lines to remember than you. Besides, you'll be a beautiful Snow White."

"Really?" Megan asked. "You mean it?"

In typical Erin fashion, she rolled her eyes. "I

wouldn't have said so if I didn't mean it, silly. Want to go upstairs and practice now? You can read all your lines to me, if you want. And you can listen to my lines, too. We'll practice every night!"

Megan vaulted off Parker's lap, already running upstairs to their bedroom. Before Erin followed, she kissed him on his cheek. "I'm sorry, Daddy," she said. "I was just really mad."

"I think you were more sad than mad," he said. "And I accept your apology, but when you go upstairs, you should probably let your sister know you're sorry. She was hurt, too."

"I will. Megan was really nice, trying to give me her part, huh?"

"She was."

"I'll tell her thank you for that," she said. "Because it was nicer than I deserved."

And right there was another lesson to be learned. "Why do you think that is?"

"Um. Because after I explained, she understood why I was so upset," Erin said, chewing on her bottom lip. "And that made her want to help me feel better. And that is why—" a grin wreathed across her face "—we never forget that we're family, and that we love each other."

"Perfect answer, kiddo. I give you an A-plus."

Erin kissed his cheek again and, for a second, rested her head on his shoulder. Someday, he knew, he'd think back to moments like this and miss them. Oh, not the fireworks or the tears, but the quiet, sweet father-and-daughter moments when the entire world became peaceful.

It ended too quickly, this particular moment. She raced up the stairs without a backward glance, intent on helping her sister and on being the best Fairy Godmother she could. Exhausted, Parker closed his eyes. Sighed. Breathed out the leftover tension from the emotional scene.

He'd had a hectic day, even before the Snow White catastrophe, and the rest of the week promised more of the same. Many of his clients wanted to finalize their marketing plans for the new year before Christmas, and daily, it seemed, he had potential new clients reaching out.

More business was always a good state of affairs, but with the holidays approaching, the start of the Christmas play rehearsals, considering Reid's request and, of course, spending time with Nicole, he expected there would be plenty of scheduling snafus on the horizon. It wasn't easy, being a single parent. Worthwhile? Without doubt. And his girls were his life.

He just wouldn't have chosen this path if he'd had any say in it at all. Two active and involved parents were better than one, especially when time and energy were at a premium. If he got sick or was in another accident, his daughters didn't have a spare parent to count on, lean on, be there for them. They would be alone. And that possibility—well, it haunted him.

Day in and day out.

Sunday morning dawned bright and cold, with a few snow flurries decorating Steamboat Springs. Nicole looked through her kitchen window into her fenced backyard, enjoying the sight of Roscoe romping in the snow. That dog had to be part moose, she decided, because he'd been out there for an hour already with no signs of getting cold, slowing down or wanting to come in.

Yawning, she retreated from the window to pour another cup of coffee. She'd slept plenty long enough last night and shouldn't be this tired, but life was gaining momentum, and her days were becoming packed, from sunup to sundown. With the play rehearsals officially starting this past week, her normal teaching schedule and several unexpected but wondrous outings with Parker, each day had been full. The best parts of her day involved Parker.

They'd taken to sharing their lunch break, eating in the school playground or as they walked the same path they had that first night, when they were searching for Roscoe. She'd shared dinner with the Lennox team at Fosters Pub and Grill on Wednesday night, and they'd all come here for pizza on Friday. Pepperoni and mushroom, without a sardine to be seen.

Yesterday, Parker had invited her to his sister's house for the twins' birthdays, and she'd planned on attending. But she'd woken with a headache and, worried she was coming down with a cold or the flu or some other bug, had chosen to stay home and rest, rather than possibly pass on her germs at a family celebration.

Parker had checked in several times, just to see how she was doing. Nice to be cared about, to have someone other than her parents or brother reach out in genuine compassion and concern for her well-being. Fortunately, her headache had passed without any other signs of illness, and today, other than her lethargy, she was back to her normal self.

A relief, for more than one reason. Parker and the girls would be here soon. She was joining them at the Steamboat Springs Winter Carnival, which was apparently the place to be this weekend and, from what Parker said, an experience not to be missed.

And if she wanted to be ready when they arrived, she needed to get moving. For the moment, she left Roscoe outside playing and took a quick shower, blow-dried her hair and opened the medicine cabinet to get her toothbrush. There they were, the two boxes of pregnancy tests. She reached for a box, ready to know one way or the other, and then stopped.

No. She do as she'd promised herself and wait out the two more days until Tuesday, which put her a full three weeks after the procedure. It should be more than enough time to trust in the results, and frankly, she didn't think she'd be able to push herself into waiting any longer.

She'd waited long enough. For so many things.

Parker. He was there, as well, solidly in the mix of her wants and desires, hopes and goals. He deserved to know about her baby plan, but until she had a positive or negative pregnancy test she could count on, it didn't seem logical to put any of this on the table.

Tucking her concerns into the corner, she finished with her hair and makeup, threw on a pair of jeans and a long, heavy sweater and coerced Roscoe to finally come inside. She filled both his food and water bowls, in case she was home later than expected, and had just put on her boots when the peal of the doorbell rang through the house. They were here.

Parker stole a quick kiss before they went to the car, where the girls were waiting. And Nicole quickly discovered that the Winter Carnival was Erin's and Megan's favorite local event of the entire year. The car ride was filled with chatter about everything they would do and see, what they wanted to eat and drink, and one question after another volleyed at Nicole.

Would she go ice-skating with them? Yes. Of course. Would she watch the dogsled race with them? Sure, that sounded fun. Had she ever tried ice sculpting? Nope, she hadn't, but she wouldn't mind learning how someday. Who would she root for at the kids' ice fishing contest, Erin or Megan? That one left her tongue-tied for a second, before she told them she'd root for them both, because she didn't have favorites, and the fun was in trying.

Honestly, she didn't think they really bought into her response, but they had arrived at the carnival by then, and with Parker and Nicole walking directly behind them, the girls let the matter drop in their excitement to wander. The snow still fell, though lightly, and Christmas music was piped into the air. There were food booths set up throughout, along with signs directing people to one event or another. And wow, there were people *everywhere*.

It seemed as if the entire population of Steamboat Springs was in attendance.

"Ready for this?" Parker reached for her hand, giving it a light squeeze. "And you're sure you're feeling better? No headache or any signs of illness today?"

"No headache." She breathed in the cold air, the appetizing scents emanating from the food booths. "And of course I'm ready for this. We'll have a good day."

"We will. The girls will keep us on our toes, but I expect they'll tire out before we do."

"Ha. I sort of doubt that," she said, nodding toward Erin and Megan. They would run forward a few feet. Stop, pivot to wait for the adults to catch up and then run ahead again. "Kids have endless buckets of energy, and look at them. They're almost jumping out of their skin."

"That's only because we just got here. They'll calm down soon enough."

"Hmm. I sense a strong amount of wishful thinking in that statement."

"Nothing wrong with that," he said, casting her a sidelong grin. And oh, what that smile did to her. She finally understood the true meaning of going weak in the knees. "I'm finding that where you're concerned, I have a lot of wishful thinking going on."

"Oh yeah?" Make that the both of them. "Tell me more."

"I'm not sure this is the proper time or place to let you in on all of my wishes," Parker teased. "But several of them involve getting you alone, with zero interruptions."

Warmth spread from her cheeks to her neck. She liked that idea. Blinking, deciding a change in topic would best serve them both, she said, "Are we heading anywhere specific, or just trailing the girls until a miracle happens and they tire out?"

"Somewhere specific," Parker answered. "We have

an order of events we follow every year. Right now, they're headed toward the kids' ice fishing contest."

"They really enter the ice fishing contest?" Somehow, she didn't see either Erin or Megan being this excited over fishing of any kind. From what she'd noticed, they weren't girlie girls, but they weren't tomboys, either. "I thought they were joking with that question."

"Yes, they really enter, and nope, they weren't joking." Parker's voice held pride. "They love anything outdoors. Always have. Camping, bicycling, swimming. Horseback riding, too, though Megan isn't as comfortable being on a horse as Erin. She'll get there."

"That's wonderful. Guessing they take after you in that department?"

"Started there, but Reid's sister, Haley, runs a camp for foster kids with her husband," Parker explained. "In the summer, the girls spend a lot of their time with Gavin and Haley, camping and fishing, horseback riding and hiking. They really enjoy it."

"We camped every now and then when I was a kid. I loved it. But we went on more ski outings than anything else," she said, thinking back to those summer nights of toasting marshmallows over a campfire and her brother telling ghost stories. "Do the girls ski?"

"Ah. Well, they know the basics, but we don't ski anymore."

"How come?"

"We just don't," Parker said, his sharp tone surprising Nicole. She heard him let out a breath, and then, "I'm sorry. That was rude. It's just that a few years back now, I took a bad fall while skiing. Put me in the hospital for months. It's not something I generally talk about."

Well, she understood that. And she now knew why Daisy had returned to Steamboat Springs to care for the girls. "No apologies necessary, Parker. I'll never expect you to talk about anything you don't want to. I'm sure you won't do that to me, either."

"Expect you to? No. Never," he said. "Hope you will, if you need to? Yes."

"I think that is how it should be."

They rounded the bend of the carnival, and up ahead, kids and their parents were gathered around the edge of a frozen lake. Erin looked over her shoulder at her father. "Can we go now, Daddy? It's right there! And I see Uncle Cole waiting for us!"

"Go ahead," Parker said. "But straight to Cole, and we'll be right behind you."

Another Foster. Nicole remembered the name Cole, knew she'd met him at her brother's wedding, but didn't have any true recollection of what he looked like. "The Fosters are everywhere, it seems," she said. "That's great, that they're so willing to help out with the girls."

"We're family," Parker said simply. "And the girls will be entered into different categories, due to their ages. Cole will help Erin and I'll go with Megan. None of the kids are allowed on the ice without an adult, for obvious reasons."

"Makes sense," Nicole said, grinning as she realized she'd given the completely right answer to the who-would-she-root-for question. She could root for them both. Separate divisions meant both could actually win. Wouldn't that be something? "Where do I go?"

"I wish you could go with Megan and me, but only one adult per child." Parker put his hands on her shoulders and turned her toward a grouping of picnic tables and chairs. "You can sit there and watch, grab a cup of hot chocolate if you want. This usually goes pretty fast."

Disappointment settled, even though she understood that rules were rules. She would've liked to have been part of the action. She sent the useless emotion scurrying into the shadows. She had the entire day to spend with Parker and the girls. Maybe longer—much longer, even—if this relationship kept heading in the right direction. The direction she wanted.

Smiling, she said, "I will grab some hot chocolate and root for both girls to win."

He kissed her then. Quickly, gently, but in those few seconds their lips touched, heat exploded into being. Would she ever get used to that? The instantaneous response he pulled from her body? She didn't know, but she hoped not. She loved how this man could do that to her, so easily, so effortlessly. She also hoped, fervently so, that she did the same to him.

For him.

Nicole got her hot chocolate, chose a seat where she could see fairly well and watched with interest as the contest began. They started with the youngest kids, taking them onto the lake and to marked-off areas where a circular chunk of ice was seemingly magically removed, leaving a hole for the child to cast their line. The first, second and third child to reel in a fish won prizes, but there were other winners, too. Prizes were given to those with the smallest fish, the largest fish, the best-looking fish and, yes, even the ugliest fish.

There were four age groups altogether. Megan and Parker were in the second group, while Erin and Cole were in the third. When all was said and done, neither Lennox girl won a prize, but both had actually caught a fish. That seemed enough to put huge smiles on their faces.

"Did you see, Miss Bradshaw?" Megan asked, running to her side. "I got a fish! Last year, I didn't, but this year, I did. He wasn't that pretty or ugly, though. Just average."

"I did see, and you know what?" Nicole tousled Megan's blond hair. "I think when we're not in school, you and Erin should start calling me Nicole."

"That seems weird," Megan said, scrunching her face. "I don't know if I'll remember."

"Remember what?" Erin asked as she joined them. Cole and Parker were with her, coming up from behind. "And what seems weird, Megan?"

"Calling Miss Bradshaw 'Nicole' when we're not in school."

"That isn't hard. It's her name, and Daddy calls her that all the time."

"Listen, girls, feel free to call me either," Nicole said. "We're spending so much time together now, I just thought it made sense. But you need to be comfortable."

"Just don't call her late for dinner," Cole interjected. "Isn't that the line?"

"I'm never late for dinner. Or dessert. Or…well, anything that has to do with food."

Cole's jaw dropped open. Looking at Parker, he said, "You met a woman who isn't a Foster, who loves to eat and has no problem admitting so? Don't let this one go, Parker."

"I have zero intention of letting her go." Oh. Just, oh. He came to her and held out his hand, which she accepted. He gently pulled her to her feet. "Cole is taking the girls to see the ice sculpting contest. We can join them or, if you're a trusting soul, I have another plan in mind."

"Another plan, huh?" The corners of her lips twitched and her green eyes darkened a shade. He could look into those eyes all day. All night. "Well, so far, I've liked all your plans," she said, "but I don't know about missing out on the ice sculpting contest."

"Go with Daddy, Miss… Oh. Um. Nicole." Megan smiled when she got the name right. Parker almost laughed at her delighted expression. "He told me the surprise and it's a really good one. You'll like it a whole lot more than ice sculpting!"

"Well, then. I will take your advice, Miss Lennox," Nicole said with a wink.

Lord, this woman made him happy. Just by the simplicity of who she was, how she behaved with his kids, what made her smile and laugh. How she made *him* feel. And he hoped she liked his surprise as much as he thought she would. A romantic moment, for just the two of them, before they returned to the girls and a day of family fun.

Was it good or bad that he was already thinking of

Nicole as part of his family? He didn't know. Didn't need to determine that just yet, either. Wouldn't even try to until he'd worked all the rest out. One day at a time, he reminded himself.

Focusing on Cole, he said, "Thanks for this. We'll catch up to you in an hour or so."

"Ah, no thanks necessary," Cole said to Parker. "We'll have a great time. Right, girls?"

"Right, Uncle Cole," Erin said. "Will Rachel be there, too?"

"That she will. In fact," Cole said, checking his watch, "she is probably there now, waiting on us. We should get going." Then, with a quick nod in Nicole and Parker's direction, he and the girls wandered off toward where the ice sculpting contest was being held.

As they walked away, Parker heard his eldest daughter say, "Tell me what Daddy's surprise for Nicole is, Megan. You can't keep it a secret from me."

Before Megan's response made it to Nicole's ears, he crooked his arm through hers, so they could walk together, saying, "So. Here's something you should know. I could barely pay attention out there on the ice, thinking about stealing a bit of time for us to have to ourselves. I'm beginning to realize it will be rough, finding that time, because of the girls."

"Oh, I think we're doing okay," Nicole said easily. "I adore Erin and Megan, and they're as much a part of this as we are. I mean, in a different way, but just as important."

"That's exactly it, but a lot of women wouldn't be so understanding of all the family togetherness, especially at this stage." Probably helped some that Nicole earned her living as a teacher. Obviously, she liked kids. Even so, "Thank you, for being you."

He wondered how she would've handled the conflict with the girls the other day over Snow White, and how the girls would've responded to whatever Nicole's method of cooling a heated situation was. Would she have gotten to the bottom of the issue? If she remained in his life, she'd eventually be there when something similar occurred. No reason to worry, to speculate now. Plenty of time. Plenty of opportunity. This, he reminded himself yet again, was not a race. Despite how strongly his intuition insisted otherwise.

"You're welcome. I can say the same. Thank you for being you," she said. "But really, I don't know how to be anyone but me, nor would I want to morph into another person. Even with...well, what I've gone through. Experiences build us, you know?"

"I know. Doesn't mean we wouldn't change certain things, if we could," he said, thinking of Bridget. Not the right time to have her in his head, but there was plenty he would change there, if he could. Like dragging her to the doctor a lot earlier. So she had a real chance.

So his girls still had their mother.

As they walked and talked, he'd purposely angled their path just off course enough so that their destination remained something of a surprise. He stopped walking, and since they were holding hands, she stopped, too. "We're here, Nicole. I hope you're not afraid of horses."

It took her a few seconds to gather her bearings, but he saw the instant her gaze landed on the row of horse-drawn carriages to their left. Tipping her head back, she opened that gorgeous mouth he couldn't wait to kiss again and laughed. In delight. In anticipation.

In, well, who knew what else, but all good. He knew that much.

"Parker! A horse and carriage ride? What a perfect, romantic idea on a snowy day."

She stood on her tiptoes, placed her hands on either side of his face and lightly brushed her lips against his jaw. With the good sense that God gave him, he bent forward and captured her mouth. She tasted of chocolate. Sweet and creamy and rich. Delectable and delicious, too.

This was Nicole. He was pretty sure this was *his* Nicole.

Her fingers stole into his hair, pushing his head down another degree, and he swore that he felt this kiss all the way to his bones. Every part of who he was ached for this woman, needed this woman, had waited for this woman to appear in his life.

And here she was.

Yeah, he was falling in love. With this woman, with Nicole. And unless he was way off base, he recognized that she was falling for him. Why, then, did he feel as if he was just a single breath away from losing her, when they'd barely begun?

And how could he do away with that fear, once and for all?

Chapter Ten

It was Tuesday morning. The moment of truth had arrived, and now that it had, Nicole almost wanted to put off peeing on the stick for another full week. Oh, she still yearned for a baby. Still dreamed of becoming a mother. But so much had changed in three weeks. Parker had entered her life, and in him, she saw the possibility of an enduring relationship.

Like the one her parents shared. Like what Ryan had found with Andi.

With Parker came two little girls. Motherless girls. And Nicole's heart had already let them in, and *their* hearts mattered to her. If she were pregnant, that very fact alone might be too much for Parker. Because he would have to accept her baby if they were to remain in a relationship, and if someday that relationship became a marriage. Well, she'd want him—no, she'd expect him—to love her child just as much as she would love Erin and Megan.

But that would also put a huge burden on his shoulders. If she were to face a recurrence. If she were to lose a second battle with her worst enemy, then Parker would have a third child to raise alone. Oh, he'd take on the responsibility and his heart was plenty big enough. Those weren't the questions. He would give her child everything he gave his girls.

But really, how horribly unfair would that be?

Parker Lennox deserved every good and beautiful and wonderful thing this world had to offer. He did not deserve to lose another woman to cancer and to raise a third child—one that wasn't even biologically his—all on his own. And oh, Nicole hated that these thoughts were swarming her brain, rather than those of a positive and hopeful nature. She *wasn't* ill.

She might not be pregnant, either. And if she wasn't, she could just stop trying for now. She could give all the necessary time to this relationship, let it grow and blossom and mature, and then, if it made sense and he was a part of the decision from the beginning, attempt to create a baby with Parker instead of a donor, using IVF, just as she was now.

But that would mean waiting even longer to become a mother.

Tough decisions, all the way around, and the longer she held off on peeing on this damn stick, the more time she had to live in limbo. Blissfully unaware. Except, of course, her brain didn't function that way, and the questions and concerns would continue to eat at her. So, as much as she wished she could wait and push this off into the distance, there was no logic there.

It was time.

Before she could talk herself out of it, Nicole unwrapped the package. She didn't need to read the instructions, as by now she knew them by heart. So, she did the deed, replaced the cover on the stick and set it on the vanity. She walked out of the bathroom to get a glass of juice, to let Roscoe outside, because she'd learned that standing there and staring at that stick was akin to waiting for a pot of water to boil. Better to do something else for a few minutes.

She let out the dog first, poured her juice second, stood and stared outside third. Did she still want this? *Yes.* That wasn't a question, either. There was just so much to consider now that this man was in her life.

Why hadn't she met him a year ago? Or heck, a week earlier than she had? Because fate didn't work that way. Easy enough answer, even if it rankled. Because everything happened when it was supposed to, not necessarily when you were ready or wanting or waiting.

Time was up. In almost slow motion, she rinsed out her juice glass and left it in the sink, turned on her heel and went to the bathroom. She stood in the doorway and breathed, reminded herself that positive or negative, nothing else could happen until she knew. Limbo didn't do anyone any good. Limbo wasn't a place to aim for, it was simply a place to wait.

Right. Limbo might sound safe and comforting, but

in reality, being stuck would cause her far more harm than good. So, she walked forward, her heart in her throat, and picked up the test. She didn't need to remove the cover to see the result, but she did, anyway. Mostly because she thought her eyes were playing the worst trick in the world on her.

Two pink lines. The positive reading she'd waited so long for that, in nine months, would equal a baby in her arms. It had happened. She was going to be a mother. Joy swept in, almost knocking her to her knees with its swiftness, with its saturating, engulfing power.

A baby. Finally.

This was one of the last rehearsals before the actual play, and Parker thought the kids were as close to ready as they were going to get. And his girls? Well, they were the most prepared. Erin had lived up to her word and had practiced with Megan every night and on the weekends. Lord, he was proud of them, of the hard work they'd put into this and how their determination was paying off. He was damn lucky to know them. Even luckier to be their father.

"They're such great kids, Bridget," he whispered. Safe enough to do so, as no one else was seated in the same row. "And they're growing up so fast. Too fast, really. I wish you had the chance to know them now, as I do. And oh, do I wish they never had to lose you."

Losing Bridget had created the biggest, deepest pit of emptiness in their lives, in Parker's life. He'd tried to deal with that emptiness in a variety of ways; everything from anger to ignoring it even existed. Nothing had proved successful. That gaping hole just kept surviving, no matter what he threw at it. So, he learned to live with the emptiness and had stopped fighting against it so hard. That had worked, to a certain degree, and had certainly given him some peace.

But every day he knew Nicole, every minute spent in her company, every kiss and every laugh and every touch, was slowly eradicating that damn empty space he'd fought for so long.

Miraculous. If a better word existed, he didn't know what it was.

At the same time, that she fit so well, that she was able to do for him what nothing else, no one else had, scared him senseless. It was an admission he'd rather not make, but there it was, the truth. How could he recognize the good, appreciate the hell out of it, but still be scared? He didn't know, hadn't quite worked that one out yet. Until he could, he figured that fear would hang around as long as the emptiness had. And that—well, that was something he couldn't accept or learn to live with. Doing so would only hold him back.

Reid had been right on that front.

Parker sighed in resignation and a good deal of frustration. He wanted everything possible with Nicole, but that damn voice in his head kept whispering she would just leave him, like Bridget had, and he would be a fool ten times over for thinking, hoping, that this time would be different. So, what was he to do about that? Go forward and ignore the voice, trust his gut knew better, or end things now, before she got sick and he watched another woman wither away?

Another woman he loved. Another woman he wouldn't be able to save.

He did not know. Couldn't even hazard a guess other than, whether by his choice, hers, or the universe's, he did not want to lose Nicole. So for now, he supposed he'd just keep doing what he had been all along: spending whatever time he could with her and hoping that damn fear would go away of its own accord. Just vanish into thin air with a puff of smoke.

His daughters found him then, rehearsals being over. They were hungry and tired, requiring his attention, but happy. Tying his questions, his concerns, into a nice, neat little bow—he couldn't answer them now, and they'd be there to unravel later—he focused on his girls.

"You're sure you don't want any help?" Nicole asked Parker for the third time. She was at his house, and assuming he managed to untangle the massive ball of twinkle lights, they would soon be decorating the Lennox Christmas tree. "I'm right here, with two capable hands."

Eyes that were more hazel than blue today met hers. "Nope," he said with that quirky-as-all-get-out grin. "I am the Christmas lights department, from untangling to stringing the tree."

She tried not to stare, but this? Not so easy to do. Especially now. His thick, off-white fisherman sweater, along with a pair of blue jeans that seemed specifically made to fit his body, gave him that casually rugged, sexy-man appeal. He even had the stubble-on-jaw thing going.

"To taking the lights down and putting them away, when Christmas is over?" she asked. "Because you know, if so, that mess you're dealing with? All your fault."

A rumble of a laugh emerged. "Yeah. I created this mess last year, in my rush to get everything dealt with before our trip to Boston to visit the girls' maternal grandparents. This year," he said, "we're not heading that way until the girls' spring break."

Would they still be in each other's lives in four months' time? She hoped so, but now that she knew she was pregnant, she had to tell Parker. Tonight. It would be one of their most difficult conversations to date, and she really couldn't guess how he would react. Shouldn't try to guess, either. Whatever happened, happened. Better to focus on *this* moment, rather than the moment, the conversation, that would come later.

Suddenly, a series of playful barks wafted down the stairs from, Nicole assumed, Erin and Megan's bedroom. She'd finally let the dog off house arrest, and upon arriving an hour ago, the girls had greeted him with such enthusiasm that Roscoe had instantly followed them upstairs.

Parker had then given her a quick tour of the split-level house the Lennox family called home. A single bathroom and two bedrooms were upstairs, one of which the girls shared and the other, naturally, was Parker's. The downstairs consisted of a large living room, kitchen, dining room and a half bath. It was a cozy house, not large, but spacious enough for a family of three.

This room, the living room, was a comfortable, bright space. Here, Parker had used vivid colors throughout, including a strawberry-red sofa and a puffy, lemon-yellow chair that was large enough to easily hold two adults. There was a low-to-the-ground, square coffee table that was perfect for family game nights and meals in front of the television, and two squat bookshelves that were filled with an array of books, photos and craft supplies. In one of the corners, a pile of pillows and folded blankets were ready for chilly nights and afternoon naps.

She loved the space. It was a room meant to gather, relax and enjoy. Made her think of her own sparse living room and the fact she'd yet to actually buy a sofa. Her house, while larger and architecturally charming, didn't have near the family appeal of Parker's. Of course, he'd lived here for years, and she'd barely moved in. She had time to create a home.

"Well, if you don't need help with that, is there anything I can do?" she asked Parker, whose sandy-blond head was still bent over the knotted ball of lights. And just that quick look in his direction ignited the need in her blood. A hungry sigh escaped. "Bake cookies? Organize the ornaments? Remember, I'm right here, with two perfectly capable hands. And legs."

"I almost got it, but I do appreciate your offer. All five of them." Another smile. "And your hands and legs are more than capable. I'd call them downright beautiful."

"Well, Mr. Lennox, if you weren't so busy…" She let her words disappear, thinking again about the conversation they had to have later. Sexual innuendos might not be appropriate until they had. Or maybe she should just be herself? "Nothing at all, huh? What about with the girls?"

Parker unraveled a particularly snarly portion of the lights before saying, "See? Almost there! And yes, actually. You could run upstairs and let them know we'll be ready to hang ornaments soon. Erin will want to make popcorn and Megan likes to pick out the music."

An easy enough task. Nicole took the stairs two at a time and crossed the short hallway to the girls' bedroom. Their door was cracked open, so she peeked inside.

It was a beautifully decorated room. Pale green paint coated the walls, along the bottom of which were the cutest multicolored butterfly decals. Fluttery pink curtains framed the two windows, both of which were long and narrow, and in the far corner, a tall shelf housed a small television, books, dolls and art supplies. Rounding out the space were the girls' beds, wall hangings of ladybugs, flowers and birds, and, of course, an impressive pile of stuffed animals.

It was a delightful room, and perfect for two girls.

At the moment, they were sitting across from each other, dressed similarly in blue jeans and sweaters— pale pink for Megan, sky blue for Erin—and were in identical poses, with their backs against the wall, their legs bent and their scripts on their knees, as they practiced their lines. Geez, she was proud of these two. They were her hardest-working students.

And Roscoe was stretched out between them, evidently worn-out from the exertion of playing with two little girls, rather than only Nicole. Erin had one hand on his head, scratching between his ears, while Megan was petting his back. He was in pure heaven.

"Hey, you two," she said as she entered the room. The girls stopped going over their lines and Roscoe lifted his head at the sound of her voice. His tail thumped once, twice, three times against the floor. "Hello to you, buddy. I see you're soaking up all the love you can."

"We do love him, and he's fun to play with," Megan said cheerfully. "Can he stay overnight sometime? And sleep in our room? Please?"

Seeing how she had no idea what Parker would say to such a request, she said, "I know Roscoe would love a sleepover, but that's something we'd have to go over with your dad."

"But if he says yes, he can?"

"Well. You'd have to be very careful, because remember, he likes to run." As she spoke, a rush of lightheadedness came over her. Not wanting to alarm the girls, she stepped back to one of the beds and sat down. That, along with the tenderness in her natural breast, were her only symptoms so far, and had started just the other day. The dizziness would pass soon enough. "But yes, if your dad is okay with it, and you are very careful, then I don't see why not."

"Oh, thank you!" Megan grinned. "Did you hear that, Erin?"

"Of course I heard, Megan. I'm right here." Then, setting her script on the floor, she looked at Nicole. "Can I ask you a question? It's about the play."

"You can ask me anything you like," Nicole said, "whenever you like."

"Um. It's okay now. I'm not upset or anything anymore," Erin said, speaking slowly, her brown-eyed gaze directed at the wall behind Nicole. "But why did you give me the Fairy Godmother part? She doesn't really do anything except talk about the story to the audience."

Nicole wasn't shocked by the question. During their carriage ride, Parker had filled her in on what had happened with the girls, and they'd decided it was best to leave the topic alone, unless one of them came to Nicole with questions. And here they were.

"That's super easy to answer," Nicole said. "The Fairy Godmother is actually one of the most important roles in the entire play, Erin. She's the narrator, and for this play, she's the first voice the audience will hear and the last. I needed someone who was really comfortable onstage, could speak clearly and…well, with personality. You were the very best person for the role."

"Really?" Erin asked. "The best person for one of the most important roles?"

"Really. And both of you are doing an excellent job." Rather than easing, the dizziness had grown worse. "I'm proud of you. Both of you."

"We've been practicing a lot." This came from Megan. "Every single day and night."

"I can tell. I really appreciate all your hard work, and I wish everyone else in the play had the same mind-set." Nicole pushed the hair from her forehead and breathed in deeply. She might need to get some juice or lie down. "Your dad wanted me to tell you that we're almost ready to start decorating the tree. Erin can make the popcorn and Megan can choose the music."

Megan jumped to a stand, put away her script and sped downstairs in all of ten seconds. Erin, however, stayed on the floor, petting Roscoe with one hand while flicking at the corner of the script pages with the other. "I guess I have another question," she said. "Is that okay?"

"It sure is. Ask away."

"You and Daddy are dating, right? Like boyfriend and girlfriend?" The words were spoken in a casual tone, and nothing about Erin's body language seemed to state she was upset.

But Nicole didn't know what Parker had told them, if anything, and she didn't think it was her place to speak for him on something so important. So, she went with "We've become good friends, sweetie. I enjoy your dad's company, and he seems to enjoy mine."

The answer seemed to satisfy Erin, thank goodness, because the next words out of her mouth were "I should go make the popcorn. Want to come with me and help?"

"I would love to help, and we can check in on your dad. See if he is still untangling those lights or if they've made it to the tree yet," Nicole said as she stood. Oh. Bad idea. The room spun and her vision swam. She sat down again, instantly, and put her head between her knees.

"Nicole, are you okay?" Erin asked. "Nicole?"

Roscoe, sensing her distress, pulled himself off the floor and sat next to the bed, leaning all of his weight against Nicole's legs. A sense of security stole in, safety. Roscoe was always there for her, no matter what. He whined, just a little, and pushed his nose into her hair.

"Yes, sweetie. I just need to sit here for a minute," Nicole managed to say. Oh, this was bad. As in, she might actually pass out, bad. "Could you get me some juice, maybe?"

"Does it matter what kind of juice? We have apple and orange and grape."

"You choose. Just…hurry, please."

She heard Erin take off at a dead run, yelling for her father. She heard Parker's voice, loud and concerned, and his footsteps as he charged up the stairs. Throughout it all, she kept breathing, kept her head between her knees and hoped she wouldn't faint.

Oh, how she hated this feeling. Of not having any control over her body.

And then, there was Parker. "What's going on, honey?" His voice was a comforting mix of warmth and strength, and just by the sound of it, by his very presence, she felt protected. Cared for. "Tell me what the problem is. What do you need?"

"I'm really light-headed. I… Wow, this is bad." She pushed out the words, feeling as if she were trying to talk while underwater. "I asked Erin to get me juice. That should help."

Roscoe whined again, pushed his nose harder into her hair. He remembered those days, in that canine brain of his, when she would sit like this, trying to quell the nausea, the dizziness, that the chemo brought forth. And he'd stay with her, like he was now, for, well, sometimes, for hours on end. This dog had been with her, every dark and tortured step of the way.

Sitting in front of her, Parker rubbed his hands up and down her calves, the warmth of his skin easily permeating the thin fabric of her leggings to reach her skin. And the warmth, the rhythmic movement, the pressure of his touch, all served to offer another level of comfort.

"Did you eat today, before coming over?" he asked. She heard the fear resonating in his tenor, and she knew he was remembering similar moments with Bridget. She just *knew*.

"I ate, yes, but maybe not enough," Then, "I'll be okay, Parker."

Erin returned then, saying, "Nicole? I have your juice. I hope apple is okay."

"Apple is perfect," Nicole said, lifting her head and accepting the juice. "Thank you, sweetie." She took a sip, a small one, and then another. When those went down okay, she drank half of what was left and waited for her body to become hers again.

"Why don't you go check on your sister?" Parker asked Erin. "And you might as well start the popcorn.

So it's ready when we decorate. How does that sound, sweets?"

"But is Miss Brad... Nicole, I mean...is she okay?"

"She's a little dizzy, is all. Nothing to worry about," Parker said. "I promise. And when she's feeling better, she'll probably want some of that popcorn."

"Oh, I'll definitely want some popcorn, Erin," Nicole said, hoping her voice now sounded steady and strong. "I'm just going to sit here for a few minutes, let this juice finish doing its thing, and we'll be right down."

When Erin left, Parker's concerned gaze locked onto hers. "Tell me the truth, Nicole. Should I be worried about this dizzy spell of yours, beyond a low blood sugar response?"

"No. Not worried, Parker. I promise."

"Okay. Then finish your juice and we'll get you something more substantial to eat," he said, obvious relief in his cadence, in his expression. "And maybe, after the tree, when the girls go to bed, we can just take it easy and watch a movie. Just us, by the light of the tree."

Oh. That sounded wonderful. Amazing. But this man's heart was so very important. The last thing she ever wanted was to cause him harm, in any way. And this dizzy spell of hers had done just that. She knew— by his question, by the stark concern and fear in his eyes—that this experience had brought at least one frightening memory to the surface, and oh, she felt bad.

He'd asked for the truth, and while she'd answered his question honestly, she hadn't told him everything.

She opened her mouth, set to tell him she was pregnant, when she clamped it shut again. The girls were
downstairs, waiting for them to decorate the Christmas
tree. There was to be popcorn and Christmas music,
and giggles and happiness. This was not the time.

So, she nodded and finished her juice and, when the
spinning room finally settled to a full stop, went downstairs with Parker. She was already half in love with
this man. Maybe more than half. She adored his daughters and could see being their—well, not their mother,
as Bridget could never be replaced—but their mother
figure, she supposed. And she would be honored.

So very honored.

Within an hour, after a hastily prepared meal of
canned soup and grilled cheese sandwiches, the Lennox team was finally ready to decorate the Christmas tree. Megan started the music, the first song being
"Frosty the Snowman," and a big bowl of popcorn sat
in the middle of the coffee table. And the girls—they
were beside themselves with excitement.

Sipping her hot cocoa, Nicole sat on the sofa and
took everything in, knowing she would want to remember every aspect of this evening. *This* was important.
To the girls, to Parker and, therefore, to her. One large
plastic bin sat in the very middle of the living room
floor. No one had removed the lid yet, and the girls,
as they played with Roscoe, kept looking at their father. Waiting, she assumed, for him to give them the
go-ahead to open that bin and start decorating. It felt,
well, a lot like the start of a marathon, waiting for the
whistle to blow.

All at once, Parker went to the front of the now beautifully lit Christmas tree and clapped his hands. Loudly. At the sound, the girls stopped playing with Roscoe and bounced to their feet. They hunched their bodies forward, their arms at their sides, with one leg just slightly in front of the other, and Nicole almost laughed—almost, because yes, this did seem very much like a marathon was about to begin. A Christmas tree decorating marathon, perhaps.

"Are you two ready?" Parker asked. "And do you remember the rules?" Both girls nodded and leaned forward another inch. "Okay, then. Get ready! Get set! And…go!"

And bam, they were running toward the bin with all their might, which was only a few feet from where they started, so it took them all of ten seconds. If that. Megan got there first, by the slenderest of hairs, and threw herself on top of the closed bin.

"Me! I got here first!" she exclaimed with a mile-wide smile. "Right, Daddy?"

"That's my official call," Parker said, grinning at Nicole. "What did you see, Nicole?"

"It was very close," she said, "But yes, Megan was first."

Erin didn't argue or try to insist on a different call, just dropped to the floor next to the bin, saying, "Good job, Megan! You beat me fair and square."

"Thank you, Erin!" Megan said. She slid off the bin. "Can I start, Daddy?"

Crossing the room to sit by Nicole, Parker nodded. "Go for it, kiddo."

Megan took off the lid and, one by one, removed smaller boxes from inside. She seemed to be looking for one specific box, and finally, she found it. And from that box, she gently—almost reverently—removed a hand-painted ornament. An angel. She wasn't that large, maybe three inches long, with pale golden hair, a sparkling halo, and clasped in her hands was a flower.

"This one," Megan said softly. "I want to hang this one first."

"Tell us why, kiddo," Parker said, his voice equally as soft. Emotional. "Why that one?"

"Because this one is the very last angel that Mommy ever painted." Megan turned the ornament over in her hands and showed the underside, where the initials "BL" were written in a black marker, along with the year. "We never choose her to go first, and I was thinking… if this is the last angel that Mommy painted, she should be first on the tree."

"I think that is an excellent reason." And as he spoke, his hand found Nicole's. He held it, tightly, as if he was afraid she'd run away. "I remember when she painted that one, sweets. She changed the hair color several times. At first, that angel had brown hair, then white, and then several different shades of blond, until she finally found the right color. That color."

The girls paid rapt attention to every word Parker said, obviously hungry to hear anything and everything they could about their mother. Nicole knew that Megan had basically zero memories of Bridget, and Erin had retained only a few. That broke her heart, not just for the girls or Parker, but for Bridget. She couldn't even know that her words, her voice, her touch would be remembered by her precious daughters. And that, well, for lack of a better word, sucked.

Without thought, Nicole put her hand—the one that Parker wasn't holding—on her stomach, thought about the life growing inside. She hoped she would never need someone to keep her memory alive for this child, but she would want that, if the need existed. She would want someone who loved her, knew her and understood her to create a picture for her son or daughter. Like Parker had for Bridget, with Erin and Megan.

It was a lot to think about. All these possibilities, good and bad.

"Can I hold her for a second, Megan?" Erin asked. "Before you hang her on the tree?"

Megan nodded but didn't speak, just handed the angel ornament to her sister. Erin turned it over in her hands a couple of times before standing and walking to the sofa. Naturally, Nicole thought she was bringing it to Parker, but instead, she held the angel next to Nicole's face.

A pair of ten-year-old brown eyes looked at the angel, then at Nicole, then back to the angel, and even though Nicole didn't understand what was going on or why, she didn't move a muscle. She barely breathed. And she certainly did not say a word.

"Daddy," Erin finally said in a hushed tone. "Mommy's last angel looks like Nicole."

Megan rushed over, to see for herself. "She does! They both have green eyes and blond hair and...and the very first time Daddy met Miss Bradshaw, she was dressed like an angel!"

"Girls, lots of people have blond hair and green eyes," Parker said. "And you know why Nicole was dressed as an angel. It was for the Christmas play try-outs. Just a coincidence."

"No, Daddy," Erin insisted. She passed the ornament to her father. "Look for yourself!"

"I'm sorry," Parker whispered to Nicole as he held the ornament next to her face, just as Erin had. Blinking, he gave his head a quick shake and traced a finger from her cheeks down to her chin. "Well, you are correct, Erin. I see the resemblance, too. But, girls, I promise you, this is nothing but a coincidence. Your mother didn't know Nicole."

Handing her the ornament, Nicole looked at the angel's face. Oh. Wow. It wasn't just the painted color of hair and eyes, which was, eerily enough, spot-on, but the angel had the same curve to her cheeks, the same full mouth, the same rounded chin.

Coincidence, as Parker had said, of course. But a strange one.

The Christmas tree lights still twinkled, and music still played—now the song was "Rudolph the Red-Nosed Reindeer"—the popcorn bowl still sat in the middle of the coffee table, but the feeling in the room had shifted from jubilant and excited to quiet and almost spiritual. Nicole thought that was okay, probably how it should be, as the girls and Parker were thinking about Bridget and how she should be here with them, helping to decorate the tree.

Breaking the silence was Parker, who handed the angel ornament back to Megan. "You won, sweets, so pick the exactly right spot for this angel."

Megan walked to the tree and stood there, as tall and straight as a little girl could, looking for the perfect place to hang the last ornament her mother had ever painted. "At the top, Daddy. I want her right at the top, so she can look down on us and see everything. Just like Mommy can."

Without speaking so much as a syllable, Parker went to his daughter and lifted her high into his arms, holding her steady while she oh-so-carefully hung her angel. Right at the top, facing front, so yes, she could see everything. *A place of honor*, Nicole thought.

Not only for the angel ornament, but for the woman who had painted her.

She had a feeling that she'd have liked Bridget Lennox. In a strange way, almost as odd as how much she resembled Bridget's angel, Nicole missed the woman, too. Even though she'd never met her, there was a connection between them. And no, it wasn't the type of cancer they'd shared, or the hell they'd gone through in their attempts to kick its ass.

It was love. For this family.

Chapter Eleven

After tucking the girls into bed for the night, Parker took a minute to gather his bearings. The day hadn't turned out quite like he'd thought. First, there had been Nicole's dizzy spell, and in the middle of that, one memory after another had rolled into his head, taking up far too much space. There he was, trying to help Nicole, and it was another woman's face he saw. Another woman's voice he heard. Bridget's illness had become front and center again.

Brought on by his crippling fear over what Nicole was going through in that specific moment. He couldn't even help her as he should've been able to, not with his mind trying to shake off images he didn't want to see, experience, ever again.

Maybe not ridiculous, given the circumstances, but

he'd overreacted. Nicole wasn't sick. She'd confirmed that with him when he asked. She hadn't eaten. She'd had low blood sugar.

End of story.

But it had taken more than a minute to get the day, the festivities back on track. More than that, it had taken longer than a minute to get his head where it needed to be. And then, Megan's choice out of the multitude of Bridget's angels—she'd always painted one or two or three each holiday season—was the very last one she'd ever finished. The eerie resemblance of that angel to Nicole had lowered the volume on the rest of the evening.

Oh, they still followed the regularly scheduled program. Erin chose her ornament next: a red-headed, brown-eyed angel that Bridget had painted the year their eldest was born. And back and forth they went, from one girl to the other, until every one of Bridget's eleven angels were on the tree. That was when Parker broke out the rest of the ornaments, when Nicole had joined in with the tree decorating, and slowly, spirits lifted.

He'd started the tradition on how they decorated their tree the first year they'd lived here in Steamboat Springs. The connection seemed important, and even though the girls were very young at the time, the tradition had stuck. Now he couldn't imagine starting their holiday season in any other fashion. It seemed right, fitting, for the girls to have that time "with" Bridget.

The day had worn Parker out, though. Through and through. And all he wanted now, all he yearned for, was some quiet time with Nicole. Maybe he'd break out a bottle of wine they could enjoy while watching a movie. They could cuddle on the couch, make out a little—or a lot—and before the night was out, perhaps he'd dispel that crippling fear.

It was a good and worthy goal. And one he'd fight for.

Downstairs now, he didn't find Nicole in the living room, so he went to the kitchen. She was there, sitting at the table with another glass of juice in front of her, and her eyes closed. He figured the day had worn her out just as much as it had him, but the sight of the juice brought along another rush of worry. Dizzy again, or merely thirsty?

She opened her eyes when she heard his approach, and smiled. "They go down okay?" she asked. The question resonated as familiar, as if she'd asked him that nightly for, well, years, rather than only once. "And I take it Roscoe is conked out with them?"

"Yes and yes," he said, taking the chair across the table from her. "I left the door open for him, so he can leave whenever he wants. Is that okay? If not, I'll go up and get him."

"Of course, that's fine. In fact," she said over a sip of her juice, "Megan asked earlier if they could have a sleepover. And Roscoe loves them more than me, I think."

"Impossible," Parker said with a grin. "He's been with you his whole life."

She tilted her head to the side. "True. So, perhaps he just has more fun with them. Can't blame him," she said with a small, barely there sort of laugh. "Two little girls smothering him with love, affection, rambunctious play and bites of buttered popcorn is hard to beat."

"There's a point." Then, because he couldn't not ask, even if he felt like a fool for doing so, he nodded at the juice. "Still feeling okay? Because if you had another dizzy spell, we probably can't blame it on low blood sugar this time."

"I like how you said 'we.'" She paused, fiddled with the glass for a second and then released a long breath. "I got a little dizzy again, yes, but nothing like what happened earlier, and I think it's partly low blood sugar, but that's not the only reason."

In a breath, he was sitting across from Bridget, after one of her first doctor's appointments. "What's wrong?" he asked, waiting to hear the worst words in the world for the second time in his life. "And why did you tell me earlier I didn't have to worry if I do?"

"Because you don't have to worry. It isn't cancer, Parker."

The knot in his gut loosened. "Okay. Good," he said. "But what's the other reason for the dizzy spells, then? And how long have you been having them? And have you seen a doctor?"

Silence engulfed the air between them for the space of a dozen heartbeats. He knew, because he'd counted his. When Nicole spoke, she did so slowly, as if carefully choosing each and every word. "I don't know exactly how to tell you this, even though I've been thinking about it all day. So, I guess I have to feel my way through it, which means I need you to please do me the favor of hearing me out before jumping to any conclusions."

That question instantly put him on the wrong side of this conversation. The defensive side. It shouldn't have, but the fact that she didn't already know he'd listen to every word she had to say, ask any questions he might have before "jumping to conclusions," well, right or wrong, it hit a nerve. But he was a patient man by nature, a master at keeping his emotions under wraps, and he cared about this woman." So, all he said was "Of course, Nicole. I'll listen to every word."

"Thank you."

More fiddling with her cup and another sip of juice before she nodded, twisted her fingers together in front of her and said, "I never expected to meet someone like you, Parker. So, what I'm about to tell you... well, I made decisions based on a lot of factors, some more important than others, but one of those factors is I did not expect to...meet someone, potentially the right someone." She shrugged and twisted those fingers tighter. "I figured I'd always be alone."

"I figured the same," he said, relaxing somewhat. "Expecting to meet the potential 'right' someone never crossed my mind. Mostly, I've just focused on the kids and work."

"But you have kids," she said. "Great kids."

"I do." Confused, he went to the fridge and grabbed a beer. Twisted off the cap and returned to the table. "And I agree with your assessment—they are great." What he thought was about to be a conversation regarding her health seemed to have turned in another direction. "Hey, this is me. You can tell me anything. Just push out the words, and like before, I'll take it from there."

"I'm trying." She pressed her fingers to her temples. Opened her mouth and closed it again. And then, finally, she said, "I really, really like you, Parker. I think…no, I know…I could love you. So when I say I didn't expect to meet someone like you, that's what I mean."

Those words did the opposite of the others. They melted him. There wasn't a better way to put it, even if he sounded like that sixteen-year-old girl again. But something was churning in that blond head of hers, something she was going to tell him that had already sent his fear meter sky-high. "Well, that's good," he said, "because I know I could love you, too. Tell me, Nicole."

"Right. Of course." She closed her eyes for a millisecond, inhaled another of those long breaths. "I'm pregnant, Parker."

Wait a minute. That wasn't possible. Unless… No. He wagged his head as if he had water stuck in his ears. "I'm sorry, but what did you just say?"

"Pregnant," she repeated. "And I'm happy—no—thrilled about having a baby. I've been trying for a while now, and I haven't known that long. That is why I'm having a problem with dizzy spells. I need to snack more, I guess."

He tried, oh, how he tried, to wrap his head around that not-so-small bit of information, but he couldn't quite get there. "You're serious about this, right? This isn't some sort of joke?"

But he knew the second he phrased the question that Nicole would never, could never, joke about something so serious. It wasn't in her.

She didn't seem to take offense, though. Just said, "Yes, I'm serious." Now her lips moved into a smile. It was as fake as the day was long, as it wasn't mirrored in her eyes. He gave her points for trying, though. "You're not the father. In case you were wondering."

Even with his confusion and the questions bopping around in his brain like rapid gunfire, he had to chuckle. She'd lightened the mood, though he doubted it would remain that way. "Thanks," he said drily, "I might have wondered, otherwise."

"Welcome. Just wanted to put your mind at ease."

Combing his fingers through his hair, Parker counted to ten and then did so again. Nope, he still couldn't make heads or tails of this. "I have a ton of questions," he said. "I'd like to ask them, but…I don't know if you're okay with that."

"I'll answer anything you ask," she said softly. "So, ask away."

Well. Okay, then. "Who is the father? Are you married, or…?"

"Of course I'm not married," she said. "I used IVF, with a donor."

"Someone you personally know?"

She shook her head. "I know he has brown hair and blue eyes. I know he's a scientist and how tall he is, what he weighs. I know his health markers, his blood type and how old he is."

Okay, okay. Everything was starting to click into place now. IVF. Anonymous donor. But what he didn't know was "How far along are you? Were you pregnant when we met?"

"I met you on a Friday, and my last procedure was the Tuesday before," she said. "So, technically, I was pregnant when we met. I just didn't know it yet."

Again, that made sense. Earlier, she mentioned she hadn't known for that long. This information relieved him. It meant she hadn't kept something so vitally important away from him when they'd kissed. Confessed their attraction. Talked about a possible future.

"You were in your twenties when you were diagnosed?" he asked, remembering their prior conversation. Bridget had been young, too, but they'd already had the girls, so neither of them were concerned about fertility issues. Their only focus had been saving her life.

"Yes," she said, looking drained. Uncomfortable. He wanted to ease her discomfort—that instinct was still there—but he had his own to deal with, and a lot to think about. "But I didn't worry about decreased fertility when I was diagnosed. I just wanted to live."

"But at some point, you decided you wanted a baby," he said, stating the obvious. "And took the necessary steps to try to reach that goal. How long have you been trying?"

"A little over a year ago, my ovarian function had dropped to the point that if I hadn't done something soon, I would've lost the chance altogether. So, I went through a round of fertility injections, to produce eggs that we could use in IVF." She said the words almost clinically, without any emotion in her voice. But she didn't fool him.

There was a ton of emotion involved in this decision.

She then went on to explain how each step, each heartbreak along the path of becoming a mother, had just pushed her harder not to give up. How she'd decided to move here, to Steamboat Springs, since this was where her parents and brother lived. So she would have support.

He listened to every word, not only with his ears, with his heart, too. But as he listened, the images in his head were of those dark days immediately following Bridget's death. The girls' confusion. Their fear. The nightmares. And that morning he'd found them huddled together in his bedroom closet, with Bridget's clothes wrapped around them—almost covering their entire bodies—and those tears that just wouldn't stop. Those awful, gut-wrenching sobs that had knocked him to his knees, and the stark realization that he was all they had left.

Just him.

Crawling into the closet with them, he'd shuffled his girls onto his lap and held them just as tightly as they held Bridget's clothes. And he cried right along with them, all that loss and pain and devastation. The fear of the past year and all he feared moving forward. Would he be enough for his girls? Could he provide them with everything they would need?

One moment after another clicked through his brain. All of them connected to the girls, to how losing their mother had affected them, to their tears and their questions, and their never-ending thirst to "know" Bridget. He then thought of that afternoon, just a few weeks ago, when Erin had exploded into tears in the back seat of the car over her belief that she'd somehow disappointed her mother, due to a role in a play. And again, how he'd held his girls while they cried. In loss and pain and devastation. It never ended. Never completely went away.

And he doubted it ever would.

With stark clarity, he remembered the skiing accident that could have ended his life, if he'd been even slightly less fortunate. The weeks spent in the hospital. The surgeries to put his body back together. And how, in that time, he realized how selfish he'd been, putting himself at risk as Erin and Megan's only parent. What had he been thinking? His job as their father demanded more than putting food on the table and a roof over their head.

His job was to protect them, to see to their welfare, to keep them safe and whole, and to let them know they were always loved. He couldn't do any of those things if he was dead. And that was when he decided to give up skiing. A hard decision in some ways, yet an easy one in others. Sure, his time on the slopes—until the accident, anyway—had always served him well. Cleared his head, energized his body, soothed his soul. Good stuff.

And while he missed the benefits that skiing had provided—a momentary escape from the demands of life, single parenthood, that chance to let everything go for a short while except the sheer thrill of the sport— the thought of getting on those slopes again…well, it didn't appeal. Frankly, it scared the hell out of him. He didn't need it; neither did his girls.

They needed him. It was as simple as that.

He'd done okay these past few years, finding a balance between work and home, family and friends. And then, in walked Nicole, shaking the very ground where he stood.

He could love this woman. Was halfway there, as it was. His daughters could love her, too, and yeah, they were likely already on that path. She was good for them, just as she was good for Parker. He'd recognized both almost right away. Yet, that crippling fear that she'd get sick again, that his path with her would merge into the path he'd already taken with Bridget, wouldn't disappear. Even that fear he'd been dealing with, trusting in his heart, in all he hoped could be.

But now, Nicole was pregnant, and here she sat, explaining all the reasons why she'd tried so hard to conceive. And he understood. He did. She wanted to be, yearned to be, a mother. Had formed decisions to help her achieve that goal, even to the point that she'd moved to a new city, for the purpose of being close to her family. He got it. He did.

As much as he could, anyway.

Except once again, the landscape had changed. Loving Nicole now meant loving another life—her child. He could do that. There weren't any restrictions on how much love the human heart could hold. But his fear had doubled, and then tripled, and now was about as high as it could get. So many things could go wrong, yet only one thing could go right.

Betting everything—his heart, his girls' hearts—with those stakes did not make any sense. And while it was wrong to question, because Nicole's life was hers to live as she deemed appropriate, with all that he'd learned, how could she purposely bring a baby into this world? There wasn't a father. If her cancer returned, her child wouldn't even have what Erin and Megan had. He or she wouldn't have another parent waiting in the wings to be there, to support, to cherish. And yeah, it bothered him that she didn't see it that way.

"You've been quiet for a while," Nicole said, still twisting her fingers. "I…I don't know what else to say, I guess. Just knew you needed to know. And…and…"

Her words trailed off, but he heard the question she didn't ask. It hovered in the air, bounced from wall to wall, and ceiling to floor. Just waiting. And it was the question he'd been asking himself repeatedly, ever since learning Nicole had fought the same disease as Bridget. That question was weightier now, for all the reasons he'd already gone though. Hearts were on the line. His. Erin's and Megan's. Nicole's and now her child's.

"Thank you for telling me about the baby," Parker said, his voice even and calm, without a hint of the battle that raged inside. "I did need to know. I…I guess I just don't know how to process this information yet, or what to do with it. That's the God's honest truth."

Green-gold eyes grew misty with tears. "That's

okay," she said. "I understand. This is a lot to take in, for both of us. And we've barely gotten started, you know?"

Every part of him wanted to pull her into his arms, crush her against him and reassure her that he was still here. That he wouldn't leave. That he would be there for her, no matter what. But he didn't. He couldn't. Not yet. It was too terrifying to take that step, too much was at risk.

The ratio, the stakes, weren't in his favor.

Chapter Twelve

Standing backstage, Nicole watched the final act of the Christmas play, and oh, she was so proud of her kids. They had done remarkably well, better even than she'd expected. There were mistakes, naturally, but none of them were huge. A misspoken word or two, a few abbreviated pauses over a forgotten line or when a moment of stage fright hit, or a giggle when someone's enthusiasm got the better of them. But really, she couldn't be prouder.

For her first production, she thought she'd done about as good a job as she could, and her kids had knocked it out of the ballpark. Now, with only a few lines to get through before the final curtain call, she was exhausted and ready to go home. Sleep. And enjoy her Christmas break. Most of which she would spend getting her house in order.

She was going to buy that sofa, finally, for one thing. Some bookshelves, and maybe a low-to-the-ground, square coffee table that someday in the not-too-distant future, her son or daughter could use for games, crafts, or to eat a snack while watching TV.

She'd also sleep a lot. Curl up with Roscoe and cry, too, she was sure, as that had become a regular occurrence over the past week. Parker hadn't reached out since that night at his house. Not with a phone call or a text or anything. She missed him terribly.

Oh, they'd seen each other around the school. He'd waved and smiled; they'd greeted each other, but nothing else. No other conversation. If she didn't know better, she could almost believe their time together had never happened, and that she'd imagined all of it. But she did know. She could still feel the connection between them, even when they weren't together.

It was there, constantly. Probably always would be there to a certain extent. Even if, well, even if the way things were now didn't change course. That was the likeliest scenario. She had to believe that if Parker wanted to talk, wanted to try to figure this out, he'd have contacted her by now. Since he hadn't, all she could safely assume was that they—whatever that meant—were over. And she didn't blame him. How could she? She'd gone and thrown a baby into an already-complicated, complex mix. But she hadn't stopped hoping she was wrong, either.

Hope, she'd decided, was only dangerous if you didn't give it wings.

The sound of applause erupted through the auditorium, shaking her from her thoughts, and when she peeked out, she saw the audience was on their feet. Oh! A standing ovation. Unfortunately, Erin-the-Fairy-Godmother had one final line as the narrator, but every time she started to speak, the constant loud clapping and hollering from the audience unnerved her, so she'd shut her mouth, wait another few seconds and try again. With the same result.

Nicole crossed the stage as quickly as she could, to get to Erin. When she did, she saw the girl's eyes were filled with tears, and when she put her arm around her shoulders, Nicole felt the trembles skittering through her slight flame. Poor kid. She'd worked so hard, practiced so long that this probably felt like a failure, and knowing Erin, the ten-year-old was blaming herself.

Well, that wouldn't do. Leaning close, Nicole whispered in Erin's ear, "It's okay, sweets. All this noise means they loved the performance. They're showing their appreciation."

"Well, I know that," Erin whispered back, her hand over the microphone. "But I'm not done yet, and they won't listen to me, and I don't know how to make them stop clapping so they will." She gave Nicole an imploring look. "What do I do, Miss Bradshaw?"

Nicole knew that she could take the microphone, get the audience to settle down and hand the microphone back to Erin so she could speak her lines. But she also knew that wouldn't go over well. Erin needed to do this on her own so she felt she'd succeeded in her role.

"Take this," Nicole said, removing the whistle from around her neck. She used it to get the kids to pay attention when they were especially excited and her voice alone wasn't enough to reach them. She'd forgotten to take it off after their final rehearsal this afternoon.

"Oh! Okay." Erin gave her a quick hug. "Thank you, Miss Bradshaw."

"You're welcome, Erin." With that, Nicole returned to her position backstage and watched Erin in action. Ready to step in again if the need was there.

It wasn't. Erin blew the whistle into the microphone three times in quick succession, just as she'd seen Nicole do during more than one rehearsal. Instantly, the audience clamor quieted.

"I'm very happy that you all like the play so much," Erin said into the microphone, her voice crystal clear. "But I am not done yet, so if you could all please take your seats so I can finish, that would be very nice. And you can clap again after. If you want."

Oh, that kid. She was incredible.

Ripples of laughter flowed from the people in the audience, but every one of them did as Erin had asked, and only then did the Fairy Godmother reappear to bring the official ending to the play. When she was done speaking, Erin stood there. Waiting, Nicole thought, for the audience to stand again, to clap again, but they didn't. They waited as well, in perfect silence.

Finally, Erin brought the microphone to her mouth again, saying, "And that's it! We're done! Merry Christmas, everyone, and thank you for…for attending our play." She paused an additional second. Then, "You can clap again now. If you want."

And just like before, the audience came to their feet in a standing ovation, clapping and hollering. This time, Erin's face was wreathed in a big, bright smile that stayed there for the final curtain call, as every cast member made their way onstage. Nicole was so proud of Erin, of all the kids, that she almost forgot she was part of the final curtain call, too.

But when she remembered, she walked onto the stage and, in an unplanned move, gestured for Erin and Megan to join her at the front. She held out her hands to the girls, which they clasped from each side of her, and then together they bowed.

It was rather wonderful.

The glow stayed with Nicole as she finished putting away the costumes and tidying up backstage. When she had picked up the last water bottle, she let out a breath of relief. There. Now she could go home and relax. Her work here was done. As she was putting on her coat, she heard someone clearing their throat from behind her. A very male someone.

A specific male at that. Parker.

She plastered a smile on her face before turning around. He was with the girls, and all three of them were bundled in their winter coats, apparently as ready as she was to go home. And the wish that she was going with them appeared. Just as big and bright as Erin's smile was earlier.

Keeping her voice modulated, she said, "Well, hello there, Lennox team. Can't get enough of this stage, huh?"

"We wanted to say thank you, Miss Bradshaw," Megan said. "Because you helped us have a really great show, and we had a lot of fun."

"Yes, Nicole," Parker said, his hooded, completely unreadable gaze on hers. "Thank you, also, for helping Erin out when the crowd went crazy. It...well, it means a lot."

Oh, where was that man she'd originally met? The one whose smile weakened her knees, and whose arms she felt so very safe and secure in? He was still there, she knew, just in hiding. And yes, she missed him. Wondered if she'd ever see him again.

"Of course I helped Erin," she said. "But really, she did it mostly on her own. She just needed a little push to figure out what to do. Isn't that right, Erin?"

Erin nodded but didn't actually talk. Just stood pressed against her father's side and stared at Nicole with sadness and something else. Longing, maybe? Maybe that.

"I'm sorry, but we have to get going," Parker said. "Reid and Daisy were here for the play, and they're waiting for us. We just wanted to say our thanks. And—" He broke off abruptly, and for a glorious second, his shields dropped. She saw the pain and confusion; it lingered there, in his eyes. But she also saw everything she always had.

Care and concern. Attraction and want. Need and desire. So yes. Her Parker hadn't abandoned the building yet. Which meant that her hope still had wings.

"How are you?" he asked. "Feeling okay? No more dizzy spells?"

"I'm feeling great," she said honestly. Hey, physically she was, if not emotionally. "And now that I carry snacks around with me, no...no more dizzy spells."

"Good. Take care of yourself, okay?"

"I am." And then, because she had to, she knelt down and opened her arms. Both girls came running, and she gave the tightest of hugs. She missed them, too. "You girls have the best Christmas ever, okay?" she said softly. "And I'll see you soon."

They were gone then, as quickly as they'd arrived. But less than thirty seconds after the trio had departed, Erin returned. This time, by herself. She rushed in, breathless, and stopped in front of Nicole. "I need to tell you something," she said, her words a jumble. "But Daddy's waiting, so I have to be fast. We're going out for pizza."

Not that long ago, Nicole would've been going with them. Silly to be sad over that. She could go home and order a dozen pizzas if she chose. "Sure, honey. Is something wrong?"

"No." Erin stubbed her boot-covered toe against the floor. "I just... Remember the angel my mommy painted?" she asked. "The one that looks just like you?"

"I'll never forget her, Erin," Nicole said, wondering what was on the child's mind. "But you know, what your dad said was right. That she looks like me is just a coincidence."

"Daddy is wrong." Erin lifted her chin a stubborn notch. "I think... I think Mommy sent you to us, and that's why she painted the angel to look like you. So we would know. And…and that's why you were dressed as an angel that night. To make sure we found you."

Nicole's heart melted and emotion clogged her throat. She leaned over and kissed the top of Erin's head. "Sweetheart, that's such a lovely thought, but… your mom didn't know me when she painted that angel. So, she couldn't have purposely made her look like me."

"She knew," Erin said. "And Daddy says when you believe in something, anything is possible. So, I believe she wanted us to find you so badly, she knew how to paint that angel."

And really, how was a person to argue with that?

A couple of days before Christmas, and Parker was miserable. Beyond belief, miserable. He couldn't stop thinking about Nicole, the baby growing inside of her, how they'd left things or how much he missed her. How much his instincts still shouted that she was "the one."

What he hadn't been able to do was extinguish his concerns, his fear, that being with Nicole, loving Nicole, would only end in tragedy. For him and for the girls. It was stupid. He knew it was stupid. There wasn't any logic there. The fear was completely based in emotional memory. That what had happened once was more likely to happen again.

A true enough statement in many cases—yes, the sun would rise tomorrow, just as it had today, as an example—but in this case? It didn't hold water, but the logic, the truth of that, hadn't seemed to gain any ground. He couldn't—just couldn't—put himself through the agony of losing another woman he loved, and he couldn't do that to the girls, either.

But everything he knew insisted she was meant for him, that he was meant for her, and he couldn't extinguish that belief any easier than the other. So, there he went, spinning in circles, going back and forth, back and forth, like a damn seesaw.

And now, here he was, standing in a pair of skis. Something he said he'd never do again. But when he'd dropped the girls off at Daisy's that morning, for a day of baking cookies, Reid had been preparing to take the twins on their first skiing expedition. Probably, Reid had planned the timing that way, in an effort to lure Parker to join them. And it had worked.

Mostly because, simply speaking, Parker didn't have the energy to argue.

It was, Parker had to admit, a beautiful day to ski. Not that he was actually skiing, but the sun was bright, the sky was a clear robin's egg blue and not so much as a flurry danced in the air. But it felt strange and uncomfortable being here, even if he wouldn't be skiing. There was literally zero risk involved, yet somehow he still felt as if he'd broken a self-made promise.

At the moment, he and Reid were in a relatively flat clearing near the bunny slope, just trying to get the kids comfortable in a pair of skis. So far, neither Alexander nor Charlotte were that interested in the prospect. They were far happier digging their hands into the snow than they were with learning how to move in their tiny skis. That was fine. At their age, just keeping the skis on their feet for more than three minutes at a time counted as a success, the goal being to orient them with how that felt so it didn't seem foreign, and to build on that in future sessions.

So, while he and Reid chatted about the holidays, work, the girls and Daisy, they mostly let the twins do what they wanted. And that gave Parker plenty of time to ponder this ongoing fight between logic and emotion, fear and instinct. Loving Nicole, even with that fear, maybe even accepting that fear was part of the bargain, or letting her go and all that could entail.

He wasn't sure why, but he kept equating this battle with his skiing accident. It was the risk, he supposed, the unknown, but also that illogical belief that if something happened once, it was likely to happen again. It was that same belief, that same fear that had led him to hang up his skis, to decide the sport held too much risk for a single dad.

But really, he'd skied most of his life. And he'd skied a lot. When that ratio was put into play, he had a much greater chance of never having another skiing accident again than he did of having a second, nearly fatal crash. Once that thought hit his brain, he couldn't get rid of it.

So, probably because of his present location, the fact that he was already wearing skis and his determination to get to the bottom of this dilemma, he kept thinking he should push against one fear in order to eradicate the other fear.

Meaning, he should follow Reid's advice and get back on the damn horse.

Adrenaline kicked in, and all at once, he decided

to go for it. Oh, he wouldn't take on an advanced run, or even an intermediate—it had been years since he'd skied now—but he could handle a beginner run. Couldn't he?

"Hey, Reid," he said, before he lost his nerve and changed his mind, before he made what could be the ultimate mistake in letting Nicole go. "There's something important I need to do, and no, I don't want to explain. But I probably need about thirty minutes. Do you mind if—"

"Go," Reid said, interrupting him. "It's the perfect day to get back on the slopes."

Of course his friend would know what he had planned. Hell, he'd probably known this would happen from the beginning, which was why he'd asked for Parker's help in the first place. Parker didn't say any of this, though, just nodded and headed for one of the beginner slopes in ground-eating—or in this case, snow-eating—steps.

He had a wall to break down, and hopefully, an amazing, beautiful future to claim. First, though, he had to prove he could ski again—and live.

Chapter Thirteen

Christmas Eve morning, Nicole was awakened by the sound of Roscoe's exuberant barking, followed quickly by the peal of the doorbell. She rolled to her side to check the time, saw it was only eight thirty and seriously considered ignoring her mystery guest. Who came visiting on Christmas Eve, before ten in the morning, without even calling first?

She closed her eyes and gave it a go, but Roscoe's barking continued, and when the doorbell rang for the third time, she hauled herself out of bed, annoyed. Today was supposed to be her day, and her plan had been to sleep until noon, watch Christmas movies, bake a pie for her parents' house tomorrow and wrap her remaining gifts.

As she walked toward the front door, she amended

her plan to include a long afternoon nap. A glance out the window, where Roscoe had decided to stand and bark, showed a U-Haul truck parked at the house across the street. New neighbors, moving in on Christmas Eve? That probably explained her surprise visitor. He or she or they had decided to come and introduce themselves. Which was fine and all. But couldn't they have waited until, oh, one in the afternoon, rather than waking her up three and a half hours before she wanted? When she actually had clothes on instead of a pair of pajamas?

Sighing, frustrated and tired, Nicole threw open the door with far more force than necessary, expecting to see a stranger on her porch. But who she saw was Parker. And oh, did he look wonderful to her eyes. Tall and strong, handsome and sure.

And that hooded gaze was gone. This was *her* Parker. She was sure of it.

"Oh. Hi there, Parker," she said, the butterflies in her stomach fluttering around at top speed. "You're up bright and early. Is…um…everything okay with the girls?"

"The girls are great, other than they're missing you." Then, as if he'd just noticed her appearance, her mussed hair and polka-dot pajamas, he winced. "Did I wake you?"

"You did. Or, rather, Roscoe did, because of you, but…it's okay."

"I'm sorry I woke you, but I had to be here early, and I wasn't sure what your plans were for today." Worry flickered over his features. "And I didn't know if you'd stick around to talk to me, if I called first. I…haven't behaved well, Nicole."

He still stood on the porch. The door was still hanging open. She was still in her pajamas. And it was freaking cold outside, so rather than respond to that last sentence, she said, "Why don't you come in? I can make some coffee and we can talk. Oh, and I have a couple of presents for the girls. I meant to bring them to the play, but completely forgot."

"Funny that," he said, a gleam of mischief darting into his blue eyes. "I have a present for you, as well. And Reid is out there, waiting to help me bring it in so he can get back home. It's a…rather large gift, so I didn't gift wrap it. I'm hoping you won't mind that."

"You bought me a gift?" she said faintly, somehow more surprised by this than finding Parker to begin with. What had he bought her? "And Reid is here… Wait. You left him out there, just waiting? On Christmas Eve?"

"He's fine," Parker said. "And as I said, he'll head home once we've…ah…brought in your present. Why don't you get dressed while we do that? And don't come out again until I say to, okay? That way, even though it isn't wrapped, it can still be a surprise."

"Um. Sure. I'll…uh…just go put some clothes on." Confused, unsure if Parker was sticking around when Reid left, Nicole went to her bedroom and sat down on the edge of her bed. He had to be here for a good reason, a better reason than delivering a gift, right?

Or, she supposed, he could be here to apologize, to ask if they could just focus on a friendship because anything more was just too much, and the gift was meant to seal the deal. Because, really, how romantic could a "large" gift be? It wasn't a pair of earrings or a necklace, a bouquet of flowers or a box of chocolates. Those were romantic gifts.

Sighing, Nicole lay back on her bed and rubbed her still-flat stomach. "Doesn't matter, baby, because I've wanted and waited and done everything I can just to have you. And while I know that Parker is a wonderful father, and that he would love you very much, and we would be so lucky to have him in our lives, we'll be okay without him."

And yes, she would be just fine without Parker. She'd get up and live her life, as she always had, tackle whatever problems came her way with every ounce of strength and hope she could muster. But with him by her side, she would be incredible. *They* would be incredible.

Well. Either way, he was here for a reason. On Christmas Eve, no less. Which meant that Parker had come to a decision, one way or the other, and whatever that decision was, she knew she'd be able to rely on his words. If all he wanted, all he thought he could manage between them was friendship, then he would be the best friend she ever had.

She did not doubt this. And that, right there, was another gift.

If he'd slayed his demons, believed in them and the future they'd talked about and had reached that miraculous decision, well, she would be able to count on that, too. He wouldn't bounce back and forth, going from one extreme to the other. Parker was reliable. Stronger than he realized, and he wouldn't promise her anything he didn't plan on delivering.

And that was when she remembered Roscoe, who, the last time she'd seen him, was barking out the living room window. Well, he wasn't barking now, and if Parker's gift required two well-built men to lift, they'd have to leave the front door open when they brought it in. Which would, once again, give her wanderlust dog a chance to escape.

Panic built in her chest. *No*. Not again. Please.

Though, she reasoned with herself and with the panic, she hadn't yet heard any commotion coming from the living room. Perhaps, her dog was still safe and sound, staring out the window. If that were the case, she did not want to ruin Parker's surprise, so she cracked open her bedroom door and called for Roscoe. He did not obey her command. Darn it all!

She went into the hallway and peeked around the corner. No sign of Parker, Reid or an extra-large gift yet, but the front door was, indeed, hanging open. She sprinted into the living room. No sign of her dog, either. Had he already made his escape?

Well, she had to find him. So, with a silent apology to Parker and his surprise, she slipped on the first pair of shoes she found and went out the front door. Yes, in her polka-dot pajamas, because she didn't take time to put on actual clothes or get her coat. When Roscoe was on the loose, every second mattered. And he'd already had plenty of seconds to get quite the head start.

He wasn't sitting calmly on the porch, naturally.

That would have been far too easy, so she half ran, half skidded down the porch steps. And okay, she probably should not have run so fast, and she definitely should have paid more attention to her surroundings, because if she had, she would have absolutely seen the slick icy spot on the walkway, and then—well, then she would not have lost her balance, and the momentum would not have sent her into a flying fall.

And oh, fall she did. In about the most ungraceful manner, too, with her feet shooting out in front of her and her pajama-covered behind smacking the walkway with considerable force. Her first thought went to the microscopic cluster of cells that would become her baby, so she sat for a second and just breathed. In and out. In and out. Other than the bruising pain in her butt, and the icy coldness of the pavement soaking through her pajama bottoms, she felt okay.

Her second thought went to her runaway dog.

Using her hands for leverage, she pulled herself to a stand and, promising herself she'd go slower, put her left foot in front of her right, and—damn it all!— slipped on the exact same patch of ice, causing her to fall a second time, in as ungraceful a manner as the first, but fortunately, with far less force. Tears filled her eyes, from the pain and the frustration.

"Nicole!" Parker yelled from her right.

She angled her head to the right, saw him and Reid on the back of that moving truck on the other side of the street, carrying a sofa down the ramp. He'd bought her a couch? The two men finished maneuvering the ramp, and as soon as they had, Parker put down his side of the sofa. He jogged over to her, his footing sound and sure, which made her a little jealous.

Why couldn't she run over snow and ice and not fall?

"Damn it, woman," he said, reaching her. "What am I going to do with you?"

Love me forever, that's what. Of course, she couldn't say that, so she went with "Believe it or not, I am okay." He ignored her statement, knelt by her side and ran his hands down her legs, to her ankles and then to her arms. "I promise. I'm fine! I just moved too fast and, as seems to be my typical when you're around, didn't see the ice."

"Does anything hurt?" he asked, running his hands over her once again.

"You mean, in addition to my pride?" she asked. "My butt is a bit sore, but other than that, I'm mostly just wet and cold. And you bought me a sofa? As a Christmas gift?"

"You need me following you around at all times, I think," Parker said, lifting her into his arms with ease and carrying her toward the house. "And yes, actually, I did buy you a couch as a Christmas gift, but that was supposed to be a surprise. What were you doing out here?"

"Sorry for ruining your surprise, and I was— Oh." She wiggled in his arms as they stepped into the house. "Put me down, Parker. Now, please. I need to find Roscoe. He got loose again, when you left the front door open, and you know how hard he is to find, so—"

"Shh, now. Don't get so upset, Nicole. Your dog is

fine." Parker carried her straight to her bedroom, where he deposited her on the bed. "I am aware of your dog's get-away-fast tendencies, so I put him in the backyard. I'm sorry you were worried. I should've let you know."

Relief centered in the pit of her stomach. She should've realized that Parker wouldn't have left the front door open with Roscoe nearby. "Okay. Good. Thank you for—"

"Parker?" Reid's voice cut through the house. "Is Nicole okay? And we still have that damn couch sitting in the street. We might not want to leave it out there, ya know?"

"She's fine. And yeah, on my way," Parker hollered back. Then, to Nicole, he said, "Get yourself into dry clothes while I take care of this, and then…can we talk? Please?"

"Yes," she said. "I mean, you just picked me off the concrete and carried me inside, plus you bought me a sofa." She grinned, fluttered her lashes a little. "Oh. And you took care of my dog. I'd say that makes you the hero of the day."

He stared at her for a second, his eyes serious. "There's so much I need to say to you."

"And I will listen to every word," she said. "Go help Reid. I'll be right here, Parker."

A sharp nod before he pivoted and left the room. While she changed into a pair of jeans and a sweater, she could barely contain her excitement. Her hope. Her belief that, yes, her future was with this man, and that he believed the same about her. It was difficult, not to ride too high on that excitement, that hope and that belief, because until she heard what he had to say, she could be wrong. She could be reading all the signs wrong.

While she brushed her hair until it shone and applied a light coat of cosmetics, she heard the men bringing in the sofa, and then, a few minutes later, the absolute sound of the front door closing as Reid presumably left. Which meant, she was all alone in the house with Parker.

Before going to him, before discovering if another miracle was in the making, she looked in the mirror, at her own reflection. She had done this daily when she was sick, when her hair was falling out, when her skin was so deathly pale. She would stare at her own reflection, look into her own eyes and tell herself that she would beat the cancer.

At the time, she wasn't sure if she believed those words every single day, but that did not stop her from saying them. From reminding herself that she was courageous enough, strong enough, vibrant enough, to make it another day, and then another, and then another, until that trail of days led her to where she needed to be: cancer free, with an entire life to look forward to.

So now, what she said was "You did it, Nicole. You made it to the other side, and you've proved how strong and courageous you are. You get to wake up every day and see the sun, shower and brush your teeth and go to a job you love. You have a baby on the way! This is the life you were after. The life you dreamed of and prayed for. And it is here."

Swallowing the sudden burst of emotion, Nicole

breathed in deeply. Yes, this life, the one she had right this minute, was almost perfect. More perfect than she had hoped for in those dark, dark days. She would remember that, no matter what Parker had to say. No matter his decision.

But maybe, just maybe, there was even more.

She found him in the living room, sitting on her brand-new sofa. He'd chosen one that was almost a carbon copy of his, but instead of red it was turquoise, which went surprisingly well with her plum-colored chairs. His legs were stretched out in front of him, his hands were clasped behind his head, and he wore that charming, lopsided smile she loved so much.

He hadn't tried to reorganize the living room, so for now, the sofa was positioned at an awkward angle in front of the chairs. It was a large piece of furniture, and she probably would've chosen something smaller, but she'd make it work.

"I can't believe you bought me a couch," she said as she joined him there, sitting directly next to him. "I love it, though. Thank you for doing this, for thinking of me."

"Nicole," he said. "All I do is think of you."

Okay, then. This seemed positive. Affirming. Hopeful. "I am sure you think of other things, Mr. Lennox. Like your daughters and work and what you're having for dinner."

"Sure, but in between all of those thoughts…is you." He turned toward her, his expression serious, his gaze penetrating. And oh, she wanted to reach over and wipe away the stress lines creasing his mouth and his eyes. "I am so sorry for how I behaved that night at my house, Nicole. I...wasn't very supportive, and I never told you how happy I am for you, about the pregnancy. Can you forgive me? So I can say the rest?"

"There isn't anything to forgive, Parker," she said, speaking the complete truth. "You were questioning, as I knew you would be, and I have some blame here, too. I should have told you that I might have been pregnant, what I was trying to do, right away."

"Oh, I don't know. I seem to remember sitting in this exact same room and asking you to let me earn your trust, before you spilled all of your secrets."

Yes. He had done that. "Well, maybe, but that doesn't change the fact that you would have had more time to process, to consider the possibility, before I just dumped it on you."

He trailed a finger down her cheek, eliciting a series of shivers that traveled the length of her body. "Okay. I'll agree we each had areas we could have handled differently, that might have eased some of the...let's go with turmoil. However, I didn't let you in, really, on the core of my struggle. I thought I could handle it on my own."

"Well, did you?"

"Now, yes, but perhaps I would've reached this place sooner. With your help."

"You can always tell me now," she said, hoping he would. Wanting him to trust her enough to drop whatever shields remained. "If you think you want to."

"I do. It's why I am here." He shrugged. "Or, I guess, part of the reason I am here."

He started to talk then, to share his experiences with Bridget, and how her death had affected and was still affecting Erin and Megan. The struggles they faced, even though they had been so young when she passed. And hearing these stories brought a fresh round of tears to Nicole's eyes and an entirely new type of pain to her heart. Those girls yearned for a mother, and they didn't even really know what that would mean. Didn't change the absence, though.

Parker sighed, closed his eyes and sighed again. He told her about his skiing accident, how badly he had been injured, and how he had processed both. His decision to never ski again, due to his responsibility to his daughters. He talked for a while about risk and fear, false beliefs and the constant fight to fill the void that Bridget had left in his life, in his girls' lives.

He opened his eyes, focused on her and said, "But then I met you. And I learned about your cancer. And this fear of losing you, of you leaving, kept playing havoc with my head. I was handling it, mostly," he said with a wry smile. "But when you shared the news about your pregnancy, this fear became a monster and—I'm ashamed to admit this—overwhelmed me."

She grasped his hand with hers. "That shouldn't shame you to admit. How could you not feel the weight of…everything, in that type of a moment?"

"Well, here's the thing. That night we first met?" he said, his voice rich and sure. "Nicole, honey, I knew I loved you then, or…I guess I knew I would love you, within minutes of meeting you. But that seemed so—" here, he laughed "—insane. So the havoc the fear created sort of merged with this intense belief, and I did not know how to handle it."

"Parker, I think I know—"

"Shh. Let me finish this, please. Because I need you to know, really know, that I am in love with you, Nicole. Completely in love with you." He spoke the words slowly, quietly, but with absolute surety. "I will love your baby, if you let me. And while I will probably never stop worrying about your health, worrying that someday you'll have a recurrence, I know if that were to happen, the only place I want to be is by your side."

"Oh. I love you, too," she said. "So very, very much."

She started to cry and shake and smile and laugh, all at once. A fourth miracle. The perfect life. Because perfection didn't mean everything went right all of the time, at least it didn't to Nicole. It meant, well, building the right team to give you the best chance of conquering the different obstacles life hurled your way. She'd always had an excellent team in her parents and brother. Roscoe, too. But with Parker, the girls and her someday son or daughter?

Her "team" was complete. Finally.

She went to him then, into his waiting arms, and his lips touched hers in a deep, searching, possessive kiss. Heat, instantaneous and intense, curled tight in her belly, and the need she had for this man, for *her* man, twisted and climbed and spread through every inch of her body. Her skin tingled. Her bones melted. And her heart, her soul, sighed in contentment.

In joy.

Epilogue

One year and one day later, Parker held his son—he and Nicole had married two months before Caleb's birth—as he watched the girls open their Christmas presents. His beautiful wife was curled up next to him, her head on his shoulder, fighting to keep her eyes open. She'd awakened early with Caleb, but she didn't want to miss a minute of their first official Lennox Christmas. And hell, he didn't, either.

The same month they were married, they made the decision to sell Parker's house and live in Nicole's. Logical. Hers had enough bedrooms for everyone, and this summer, they were going to renovate the large room on the second floor, with the help of Nicole's parents, and turn that into the master bedroom. That way, the girls could have separate rooms.

Something that Erin wanted, but Megan—well, their youngest daughter wasn't entirely sure. Parker figured she'd grow into the idea, and if she didn't, they'd give her plenty of time to adjust. Yawning, he brought his boy to his shoulder and kissed him on his downy, sweet-smelling head. Just as with the girls, there wasn't a damn thing Parker wouldn't do for his son.

And Caleb was his. Had been all along, really, even if Parker had needed a bit of time to set matters straight in his head. The choking fear that he'd almost given in to was completely eradicated now, for which he was ever grateful. Oh, as he told Nicole a year and a day ago, he'd never stop worrying about her health. But that was normal. Expected.

She was, after all, his to take care of.

Roscoe, leaving his spot by the girls, came over and whined at Nicole, doggy sign language for "Let me out, please." His wife sighed as she stood, and the look of her, rumpled and sleepy and beautiful, reminded him again of what he could've lost. Not due to cancer, but to his own stupidity. Thank the good Lord, he'd come to his senses.

Even if it had taken his stubborn best friend and a pair of skis to get the job done.

That solitary run had served its purpose. When Parker reached the bottom, all he'd felt was exhilaration for being alive. He'd taken that exhilaration, the freedom he'd gained from that run, and opened his arms to the future he'd seen with Nicole from the very beginning.

Leaning over, Nicole gave him a quick kiss that

promised more, later when the kids were asleep. She brushed her finger over Caleb's pudgy cheek and kissed him, too. She went to the girls, tousling their hair with a hand, before following Roscoe to the back door.

Yes, Parker was one lucky man.

His eyes found Bridget's final angel where it hung on their tree and his heart tugged, just a little, at the memory of his beloved first wife. She was also a part of this family; always would be. Nothing would ever, could ever, change that. Thinking of her now, he sent her a silent "Merry Christmas," and while it was a ridiculous thought, he also thanked her.

For sending them Nicole.

* * * * *

If you loved this book, check out previous books in Tracy Madison's THE COLORADO FOSTERS *series:*

A BRIDE FOR THE MOUNTAIN MAN
FROM GOOD GUY TO GROOM
ROCK-A-BYE BRIDE
DYLAN'S DADDY DILEMMA

Available now wherever Mills & Boon Cherish books and ebooks are sold!

MILLS & BOON®

Cherish ™

EXPERIENCE THE ULTIMATE RUSH OF FALLING IN LOVE

A sneak peek at next month's titles...

In stores from 16th November 2017:

- **Married Till Christmas** – Christine Rimmer *and* **Christmas Bride for the Boss** – Kate Hardy
- **The Maverick's Midnight Proposal** – Brenda Harlen *and* **The Magnate's Holiday Proposal** – Rebecca Winters

In stores from 30th November 2017:

- **Yuletide Baby Bargain** – Allison Leigh *and* **The Billionaire's Christmas Baby** – Marion Lennox
- **Christmastime Courtship** – Marie Ferrarella *and* **Snowed in with the Reluctant Tycoon** – Nina Singh

---

Just can't wait?
Buy our books online before they hit the shops!
www.millsandboon.co.uk

Also available as eBooks.

MILLS & BOON®

EXCLUSIVE EXTRACT

With just days until Christmas, gorgeous but bewildered billionaire Max Grayland needs hotel maid Sunny Raye's help caring for his baby sister Phoebe. She agrees – only if they spend Christmas with her family!

Read on for a sneak preview of
THE BILLIONAIRE'S CHRISTMAS BABY

'Miss Raye, would you be prepared to stay on over Christmas?'

Oh, for heaven's sake…

To miss Christmas… Who were they kidding?

'No,' she said blankly. 'My family's waiting.'

'But Mr Grayland's stranded in an unknown country, staying in a hotel for Christmas with a baby he didn't know existed until yesterday.' The manager's voice was urbane, persuasive, doing what he did best. 'You must see how hard that will be for him.'

'I imagine it will be,' she muttered and clung to her chocolates. And to her Christmas. 'But it's…'

Max broke in. 'But if there's anything that could persuade you… I'll double what the hotel will pay you. Multiply it by ten if you like.'

Multiply by ten… If it wasn't Christmas…

But it was Christmas. Gran and Pa were waiting. She had no choice.

But other factors were starting to niggle now. Behind Max, she could see tiny Phoebe lying in her too-big cot. She'd pushed herself out of her swaddle and was waving her tiny hands in desperation. Her face was red with screaming.

She was so tiny. She needed to be hugged, cradled, told all was right with her world. Despite herself, Sunny's heart twisted.

But to forgo Christmas? *No way.*

'I can't,' she told him, still hugging her chocolates. But then she met Max's gaze. This man was in charge of his world but he looked...desperate. The pressure in her head was suddenly overwhelming.

And she made a decision. What she was about to say was ridiculous, crazy, but the sight of those tiny waving arms, that red, desperate face was doing something to her she didn't understand and the words were out practically before she knew she'd utter them.

'Here's my only suggestion,' she told them. 'If you really do want my help... My Gran and Pa live in a big old house in the outer suburbs. It's nothing fancy; in fact it's pretty much falling down. It might be dilapidated but it's huge. So no, Mr Grayland, I won't spend Christmas here with you, but if you're desperate, if you truly think you can't manage Phoebe alone, then you're welcome to join us until you can make other arrangements. You can stay here and take care of Phoebe yourself, you can make other arrangements or you can come home with me. Take it or leave it.'

Don't miss
THE BILLIONAIRE'S CHRISTMAS BABY
by Marion Lennox

Available December 2017
www.millsandboon.co.uk